NAOMI

The Strawberry Blonde
of Pippu Town

By Karmel Schreyer

GREAT PLAINS FICTION

Great Plains Fiction
An imprint of Great Plains Publications
3 - 161 Stafford Street
Winnipeg, Manitoba, Canada
R3M 2X9

Design & Typography by Taylor George Design.

Printed in Canada by Kromar.

CANADIAN CATALOGUING IN PUBLICATION DATA

Schreyer, Karmel, 1964 -
Naomi: the strawberry blonde of Pippu Town
ISBN 1-894283-05-8
I. Title.
PS8587.C487 N36 1999   jC813'.54   C99-920101-8
PZ7.S379352 Na 1999

*For my best friend, D.P.,
and the one I can't wait to meet.*

*The story of Naomi could not have been written without the participation
of Nadya Kamienski, Junko Funaki, Masako Hiraki,
Lorri Podolski and Margo Goodhand. Thank you so much for your support
and encouragement, invaluable Japanese insights, informative Ukrainian
e-mail, and skilled editing.*

Contents

Japan

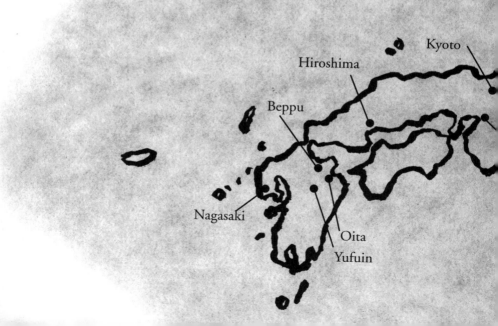

Kyoto

Hiroshima

Beppu

Nagasaki

Oita

Yufuin

A New World – Japan

The young girl awoke with a start to the sound of a crow. Bleary-eyed, heart pounding, Naomi sat up and realized that the bed – the whole room – was unfamiliar to her. Her mounting confusion subsided as she saw her mother soundly asleep on the bed beside her. In the dim light that peeked through the curtains, Naomi gazed at the beds upon which she and her mother were lying: soft mattresses laid directly on the floor, covered with billowy down-filled comforters.

And it can't even be called a floor, she thought as she wrinkled her nose. *Last night, mom called it a "tatami."* A wave of loneliness swept over her. She hugged her legs. "Why did you bring me here, mom?" she whispered to her sleeping mother, and rested her head on her knees.

As a second crow answered the call of its friend, Naomi rolled off her mattress and padded across the small room to the window. Dawn was always her favourite part of the day, a quiet time when she could think secret thoughts and try to guess what surprises the day would bring. But this morning, she could only feel the knot in her stomach, a feeling of dread and uncertainty. It was a strange feeling for her.

Naomi shook her head, trying to get rid of the fogginess in her brain. She hadn't slept well at all. Jet-lag, which she had never before experienced, had caused her to wake up at three in the morning, and it had taken her a long time to fall back to sleep. She was still exhausted after the trans-Pacific flight from Vancouver, and then another flight from Tokyo to Asahikawa in Japan's northern island of Hokkaido. She and her mother had arrived late the night before, and it had been too dark to see her new surroundings.

As she drew back the curtain, Naomi gasped, momentarily forgetting the feeling of dread and weariness inside her. A vast patchwork of green fields stretched out before her, rising up at the back against a wall of tree-covered hills, green-blue in the hazy August air. The morning light was beautifully tinted; a peachy shade that held the promise of the sun, which would soon be emerging. Naomi had never seen anything like it. She had never seen the dawn rise over hills. And she had never imagined a wall of green that could block the flat line of the horizon. Where she came from, the farming town of Portage la Prairie in Manitoba, Naomi greeted each new morning with her eyes on a distant horizon, as flat as could be. "God used a rolling pin when he made Manitoba," her grandma liked to say.

Naomi's thoughts turned to her grandparents, affectionately called "Baba" and "Gigi," meaning grandma and grandpa in Ukrainian. They had come to Canada from Ukraine many years ago. They settled in Portage la Prairie, becoming pioneer farmers on the Canadian prairie. Naomi thought about the farm she, her mother, and her grandparents had lived on together for the last two years; the wheat and potato fields, the big vegetable garden, the big old barn that needed painting. She looked up at the sky and thought of her ballet classes, her two best friends, and her school. She thought about Billy, her beloved golden retriever, and felt her heart would surely break. And in spite of the sea of green and the dawn before her, a tear rolled down her cheek.

At that moment, her mother, Sara, crossed the small room and put her arm around Naomi's thin shoulders. She drew back the curtains and the early morning light filled the strange little bedroom. "Ballet pink, isn't it, Naomi?" the woman said, and wiped the tear from her daughter's cheek. "Just like it is on the farm."

Naomi turned and hugged her mother, her body shaking with silent sobs. "I miss Imee and Lois. I miss Billy. I miss Baba and Gigi. Oh, mom, why did we have to come to Japan?"

The woman held the girl close and looked out, sadly, towards the not-too-distant hills. "Naomi, I'm sorry that this has made you so unhappy. But you know, things haven't been easy since your father and I got divorced. I just didn't want to keep living with your grandma and grandpa, after all they've done for us, all the help they've given me. I felt that it was time – "

"But I love Baba and Gigi!" Naomi interrupted. "I miss Billy and Imee and Lois. I miss my friends. I miss Manitoba." She tried hard to swallow the lump in her throat.

"Please, Naomi," her mother pleaded, and drew back so that she could see her daughter's face. "Try to understand. We can't live with my parents forever. We were lucky that they were there for us after the divorce, when I was just getting back on my feet, trying to make a life for us. But when I got laid off, I knew that it wouldn't be easy to get another job there. I knew we would have to leave – sooner or later."

Sara gently lifted her daughter's chin and looked into her eyes. "Naomi, I was lucky to get this job teaching English at the Medical College in Asahikawa. It's what I went to university for. And it'll give us a nest egg – a head start. Just one year, Naomi, okay? Just one year." After a brief pause, she continued, "We're a team, remember? We'll help each other get through this." She smiled a small smile. "Besides – look at that sky."

Naomi and her mother stood silently, hugging each other close and studying the landscape as it changed, moment by moment, in the growing morning light. Naomi tried to feel the excitement she knew her mother was feeling. *Not even the sky can cheer me up today – not for long, anyway*, she lamented. But she knew that her mother was lucky to get the job in Japan. And she and her mother were a team, she reminded herself. They needed each other. She turned to face her mother, and forced a smile. "Okay. As long as we're together, we'll be okay."

Sara squeezed Naomi tightly. "My brave girl. You've been through so much. Just one year, Naomi. And you'll be so busy here, you won't have time to think about home; making new friends, learning a new language – learning all about Japan."

A quiet knock on the door interrupted her. "Sara-san. *Ohayo*."

Naomi's mother quickly stepped across the room and opened the door. "*Ohayo*, Keiko-san," she said, using the special term for adults, *san*. Before her stood an older Japanese woman, wearing a white apron

13

over a flower-print summer dress. On her feet were matching house slippers. Her greying hair was pulled back in a tight bun and her eyes were merry and alive despite the early hour.

"I knew you'd be awake, Sara-san. You told me your daughter enjoys the morning." Keiko continued as she smiled over at Naomi, "I have made a typical Japanese breakfast for you. I hope you like it – *miso* soup with tofu, some rice, and *natto*. But I can make some toast, if you like."

"*Miso* soup and rice is perfect, Keiko-san," replied Naomi's mother. "I can't wait to eat Japanese food again. I've cooked Naomi more than a few Japanese meals over the years. You like Japanese food, don't you Naomi?" Naomi saw that her mother was looking at her expectantly.

"Yes," Naomi replied shyly. She thought of the different kinds of Japanese foods her mother had made for her over the years, and all her stories about her life in Japan after graduating from university. Naomi's mother had lived for two years in southern Japan, on the island of Kyushu, as an assistant English teacher in a Junior-High School. As the only foreigner in a small farming town of eight thousand, Naomi's mother had quickly learned to adapt to the Japanese way of life. She had to learn to speak a new language, and her neighbours were eager to teach her the necessities of Japanese life; how to cook and shop, how to mail a letter and go to the bank. Everything had been new for her. In many ways, she'd felt like a child learning all over again. Naomi had never tired of hearing her mother's stories about her life in Japan.

It was in Japan that Naomi's mother and father had met and become engaged. He had also been an English teacher in a city not far away. There were not many foreigners in the part of Japan where they lived, and the two Canadians would sometimes meet in the city to share their experiences. After two years they returned to Canada and married. But the marriage ended in divorce when Naomi was ten years old, and she and her mother went to live with Naomi's grandparents. Now, Naomi found herself in a small town in northern Japan. She thought wryly to herself, *I've always wanted to visit this country, but I never thought I'd end up living here!*

"Naomi. Naomi. Where are you?" her mother was gently shaking her shoulder and laughing. "Your mind just wandered away on us!"

Keiko smiled and said, "Come, Naomi-chan, let's eat some

breakfast. Then we will go take the train to a nearby town in the countryside. There's so much to see. And it's such a beautiful day."

"Don't forget your slippers," Sara reminded her daughter as she stepped into her own quilted cotton slippers. In Japan, people always removed their street shoes when they entered a house, and put on house slippers. Naomi dutifully slipped on the pair Keiko had given her late the night before and followed the two women downstairs.

Keiko's small kitchen was filled with unfamiliar smells. Naomi could recognize the thick, starchy smell of the rice as her mother ladled it into three small bowls. But the pungent, salty aroma of *miso* as it simmered in the soup was too much for her. She decided she didn't have much of an appetite, and secretly wished her mother had taken up Keiko's offer of toast. Naomi saw three more small bowls on the dining table, filled with something grey and lumpy. Naomi drew closer to get a better look, and her nose was assaulted by a terribly rotten smell! She lurched backwards in disgust.

"What's that!" Naomi grimaced, pointing at the mysterious smelly stuff.

Sara shot her a glance, and Keiko turned to see what was the matter. Keiko smiled patiently, "Oh, that's *natto* – fermented soy beans. It's very good for your health. Japanese people like it very much – especially with a little raw egg or mustard on top. You have never tried it?"

Sara quickly answered for her daughter. "Well, I can't say it's as popular in Manitoba. *Natto* is not easy to find."

Keiko smiled at them both as she motioned for Naomi to take a seat at the table. "Please sit down and I'll get the tea. Would you like *ocha* or *kocha*, Naomi-chan?"

"That's Japanese green tea or Western-style tea," Naomi's mother explained.

"Japanese tea, please," Naomi replied shyly, trying to be polite. Keiko smiled back approvingly. She poured three cups of green tea as Sara took her seat.

Keiko reached for her cup of tea. "I am going to make a toast," she began. "Sara-san, welcome back to Japan. It doesn't seem like such a long time ago, you were a young lady working with me in Kyushu. You became like a daughter to me. I was sad to see you return to Canada. But now you have come back to Japan – and this time you have brought your daughter with you. I am so happy to have you both here." Keiko looked at Naomi and raised her teacup with both hands. Naomi and her mother did the same. "To Sara-san and Naomi-chan. I hope you will consider Japan, and Pippu-cho, like your home."

"*Kampai* – cheers," Naomi's mother said.

"Cheers," Naomi mumbled. She smiled weakly across the small table at her mother and Keiko. Inside, her feelings were a jumble of loneliness, fatigue and anxiety. She looked down at the bowl of smelly, slimy *natto* in front of her and began to really feel sorry for herself. *Can I really consider Japan my new home?* Naomi wondered. And then she realized that, like it or not, Japan was her new home for the next long year, far away from Manitoba. Far away from Baba and Gigi, her friends Imee and Lois, her dog Billy, and the big prairie sky.

Lavender Ice Cream and Anne of Green Gables

"We're going to a small town called Furano. There are a lot of interesting things to see there," Keiko explained cheerfully.

Naomi was barely listening. She leaned her head against the window of the train and watched the fields pass before her eyes. There were familiar-looking potato fields and corn fields, just like in southern Manitoba. But scattered among them were the neat, dark green rows which Naomi now knew were rice paddies. *This looks kind of like Manitoba, but different, too – more hilly,* she thought. She found a small comfort in finding similarities between this strange new land and her home in Canada. *Maybe this is what Alberta looks like,* she speculated. Naomi had never been to Alberta, but she knew about the lovely rolling hills in that province, where the great Canadian prairie ended, and the Rocky Mountains began.

"Furano is famous in Japan for its fields of lavender. Look! You can see some over there – we are getting close to Furano, now." Keiko pointed to a patch of pale purple on the hillsides in the distance. The fields became more numerous as they approached the town, and Naomi looked longingly at the beautiful purple colours.

Sara read her daughter's thoughts. "Naomi, doesn't it remind you of the flax fields in Manitoba? It's the same colour – just more thick

17

and, well, maybe a little brighter."

There were other flowers as well; yellow tulips, red poppies and sunflowers – Naomi's all-time favourite flower. She gazed at the field of sunflowers, thousands of big brown faces all lifted towards the sun. She let her mind drift to the time, just one week earlier, when she and Gigi were driving down the Trans-Canada Highway, near Portage la Prairie. Naomi had spied one small sunflower, standing alone on the gravelly shoulder of the highway. "Stop the car," Naomi had said, and Gigi, with his amused smile, was quick to obey. Gently, she had pulled the sunflower by its roots out of the shallow soil. Later, she had replanted it in Baba's garden. *It was only a week ago,* Naomi thought. How long ago it seemed! She wondered how that sunflower was doing in its new home.

"Such lovely colours, all of them. And sunflowers, too!" Naomi heard her mother say.

"Yes," Naomi heard herself reply. But it could very well have been someone else talking, she felt so far removed from everything around her. The knot in her stomach had returned full force. Naomi sighed. She wanted, more than anything else, to go home.

"Furano. Furano," Naomi heard the conductor announce as the train rolled to a stop at a small train platform.

"Let's take the shuttle bus to 'Highland Furano,'" Keiko said, and motioned to a bus parked just outside the train station entrance. "That's where some of the biggest flower fields are."

Within minutes, the bus was parked at a large log house set among neatly manicured gardens. At one side was a large patio with tables. Beyond it, fields of all colours; red, white, yellow, and the lovely purple, stretched into the hills. Naomi sniffed the air. It was a heavenly scent.

"What's that smell?" she asked, instantly feeling a little bit brighter.

"That's the lavender, Naomi. Isn't it incredible?" her mother replied, and swept her arm across the purple fields. She took a deep breath. "Hmmmm. Let's go for a walk."

Naomi, Sara and Keiko strolled to the crest of a hill, then returned to the log house for a drink and a look at the souvenir shop. Naomi was browsing through the postcard rack when she noticed a small boy holding a pale purple ice-cream cone. She had never seen such a gorgeous colour for ice cream. She smiled at the boy's confused look as he tried to figure out what to do about the melting purple dripping slowly down his hand. The boy's eyes met Naomi's and widened in shock and surprise. He grabbed onto his mother's dress and hid behind her legs, momentarily forgetting about his ice-cream dilemma. Naomi watched as the boy's mother scolded him for getting ice cream on her dress, and roughly wiped his sticky hands with a tissue.

Naomi spotted the ice-cream seller. She wanted a cone, but was afraid to ask for it. She hesitated by the postcard rack for several minutes. The palms of her hands felt clammy. Then, summoning her courage, she walked over to the woman. "*Kore o kudasai* – This, please," Naomi said. It was pretty well all she knew how to say in Japanese, other than hello and thank you. Naomi pointed to the picture of the ice-cream cone. She noticed the sign that had the number 100 written on it and looked in her change purse for a coin that had one hundred on it as well.

The woman smiled and patted one large purple scoop on a sugar cone. "*Dozo*," she said as she handed it to Naomi.

"*Domo arigato*," Naomi replied. She turned and saw her mother watching her with a smile on her face, waving a finger in mock reproach. Naomi grinned back mischievously as she took a bite of the lovely pale purple ice cream. At once, the smile on her face flipped into a grimace. The flavour was not at all what Naomi had expected. "What is this?" she asked, holding the cone in front of her and examining it.

Naomi's mother came over and read the sign, written in the Japanese script called *katakana*. She looked over at Naomi and laughed. "Did you think you were buying grape-flavoured ice cream?" she asked, thoroughly amused by the look of confusion on her daughter's face.

"What is it?" Naomi asked. "It tastes – soapy."

"It's lavender ice cream," Sara replied, then added, "Here – give it to me. I want a try."

Naomi pulled back. "No way. That's gross, mom. Buy your own." She took another tentative lick, paused thoughtfully, then took another. "Actually, it's not so bad, once you know what it is." She smiled. "Lavender ice cream – that's a first."

Keiko joined them. "If you like lavender ice cream, Naomi, you might also like *ocha* – green tea – flavoured ice cream."

"*Ocha* ice cream?" Naomi asked incredulously. *Ocha* was a bitter tea. You didn't add sugar to it like you do with normal tea. "How can it taste good?" She wrinkled her nose and said, "I'll bet it tastes awful."

Keiko smiled patiently. "Keep an open mind and give things a try, Naomi-chan," she said, then added, "But *ocha* ice cream will have to wait for another day. You don't want to spoil your appetite." She pointed to a large bus parked in the lot in front of the log house. "There's a shuttle bus going to another interesting place in the next town. We'll have lunch there."

Naomi, her mother and Keiko got onto the bus with several other families. All of the children looked very excited. Soon, Naomi saw a sign written in Japanese, with some English written on it as well: Welcome to Canadian World – Green Gables House. She gasped in surprise.

Sara smiled, "You see, Naomi? Canada is never too far away."

"Well, I don't want it to be," Naomi replied. "But I never thought I'd see a Canadian theme park in Japan." Just seeing those words on the sign, written in a language she could read, cheered her up a lot.

Naomi couldn't wait to get inside the gate. The theme park was enormous. She could see a small locomotive train parked by a man-made lake. Running along one side of the lake were about twenty old-fashioned-looking buildings. In the middle of this neat row of buildings was a huge maple leaf built into the boardwalk in red stone. Naomi ran to stand right in the middle of the big red maple leaf. In a funny way, it made her feel like she was still in Canada. It was a silly thought. For a moment, she giggled at her foolishness, until she felt the knot in her stomach returning. *I'm not in Canada. I'm just standing on a maple leaf in some dumb theme park in Japan,* she thought bitterly. Tears stung her eyes and she lifted her head to the sun and squinted to keep the tears from coming out, before Keiko and her mother caught up with her.

They boarded the miniature train which took them to the village named for Anne of Green Gables. Naomi looked at the familiar white house with the green roof and gables. Next to it was a church; "Anne's Church," it was called. There was also a museum which had a display about the life of the author of the famous "Anne" series of books, Lucy Maude Montgomery. Naomi walked to a signpost. It was all in Japanese except for the words "Haunted Wood." She was fascinated. Naomi loved the "Anne" books.

Naomi, Sara and Keiko were walking up the pathway to Green Gables when a group of Japanese tourists came out the front door of the house, led by a red-haired girl in a straw hat, a long grey dress, and black lace-up boots! The girl spotted Naomi and smiled brightly as she came closer.

"Welcome to Green Gables. I'm Anne Shirley," the girl said to Naomi. She stopped to pose for photographs with the group of tourists. Two little Japanese girls shyly held out autograph books to Anne, who grabbed them and signed her name with the aplomb of a seasoned movie star. "Goodbye! Thank you! Please come again! *Sayonara!*" she said, and waved cheerfully as the crowd made its way to the Haunted Wood. Anne Shirley turned her attention to Naomi again. "Wow! There aren't too many *gaijin* that come to this place. Where are you from?"

"I'm from Portage ... I'm from Manitoba," Naomi stammered. "What did you call me – *gaijin*?"

"Oh, it just means foreigner; outsider, really. Some *gaijin* think it's not a very polite word, but we all use it." Anne waved a hand in front of her face. "Gee, it's hot." In a flash, she removed her straw hat, and with it, the thick orange wool braids that were her hair. Naomi gasped at the girl's real hair, all frizzy and brown.

"No, they aren't real," the girl said, shaking the straw hat so the orange wool braids flopped around. "And my name's not Anne Shirley – it's Megan Brown." She wiped her forehead with a handkerchief and put the hat back on, grinning sheepishly. "I shouldn't be taking this off in public."

Naomi laughed. It was all so unreal! "Where are you from?" she asked.

"Me? I'm from Nova Scotia. Cape Breton. My mom works in the bake shop and my dad is the blacksmith." Megan took a step closer and whispered conspiratorially to Naomi. "The Canadian World people were hoping that we were from Prince Edward Island, so we told them we were."

"Do you live here?" Naomi asked.

"No," Megan laughed. "We live in Ashibetsu, a town nearby. We've been here for three months. We'll be here for a year."

"But what about school?" Naomi asked.

"Oh, well, I've taken the year off. We decided this was an experience that we couldn't refuse," Megan said. "I'll be Anne of Green Gables for a year, then we'll go back to Nova Scotia, I suppose." She flashed Naomi a look and added, "Besides, I like being famous. I've been in the newspapers back home, and on TV here in Japan – even though I don't know what they're saying. This place is neat!" Naomi saw that Megan's face was filled with happiness.

"Don't you miss your home – your friends?" Naomi asked timidly.

Megan gave Naomi a level gaze. "Yes I do, sometimes. But they'll be there when I get back. And I'll have lots to tell them."

Naomi wondered how Megan could be so philosophical. How could she just leave all her friends behind?

"I have to go," Megan said abruptly. "Goodbye – I don't even know your name ..."

"It's Naomi."

"Well goodbye, Naomi. Enjoy Japan. It's great fun. A different world – totally!" Megan adjusted her straw hat and tucked in some loose wisps of hair. She dashed down the sidewalk, leaving Naomi, her mother and Keiko staring after her in disbelief.

"That was weird," said Naomi.

"Living far away from home means that there are surprises every day," Sara commented as Anne Shirley skipped off towards the Haunted Wood. "But I have to say that this was one of the more surreal moments."

Keiko laughed. "I have to agree with you."

Naomi was silent. Megan seemed so sure of herself. She wondered if she would ever feel so self-assured in this strange place.

Upstairs in her room that evening, Naomi got out the laptop computer that she and her mother shared. "Thank goodness for e-mail," she said under her breath as she began to type:

Email to: schulz@goforit.mb.net
From: nazarevich@arc-net.jp
Subject: I miss you!

Dear Lois,

Well, I've been here for 24 hours. I miss you and Imee so much! The lady that mom and I live with (her name is Keiko, but we call her Keiko-san) is nice, but this place is so weird. They sleep on the floor in Japan, on grass mats called tatami. And you can't EVER wear your shoes inside the house. You have to wear slippers. They eat ice cream made from green tea and lavender! And I have to learn how to use chopsticks better or I will starve to death!! Even the toilets have all these weird buttons beside them, but I don't touch them because everything is written in Japanese and I can't understand any of it.

What am I going to do? I'm stuck here for a whole year! This was mom's idea and I am tired of being pushed around.

Love, Naomi.

PS Please share this letter with Imee. Tell her I'll write her soon.

PPS Don't forget me!

Attitude Adjustments

Naomi didn't want to get out of bed. She opened her eyes and focused them on the calendar by the door. The nine large X's that she had crossed over each day since her arrival in Japan were easy to see. "Ten days – three hundred and fifty-five to go," she said quietly. Naomi calculated that if it were morning in Japan, that meant it was evening in Manitoba. She let her mind drift to a summer night on the prairies. She loved the way the summer sun in Manitoba would set slowly, and then seem to suspend itself just beneath the horizon. The horizon would glow for hours after the sun had disappeared, until it was no more than a thin neon line, before being snuffed out for the night. There was none of that here in Pippu-cho. The mountains were always there, getting in the way.

What would Baba and Gigi be doing now? Naomi wondered. *Imee and Lois?* Naomi knew Billy would be curled up by the kitchen door. A smile played across her lips as she thought of her beloved golden retriever. At that moment, a big black shadow swooped past her bedroom window. From the corner of her eye, Naomi saw only a shapeless darkness, and her body went rigid. She heard the sound of a crow. It was so loud, she felt sure it was sitting on the big tree shading the second-floor balcony.

"Shut up, stupid crow!" Naomi shouted at the window. The crow responded with another loud morning *caaw*. She tried to muffle the sound of the bird by putting her head between two pillows, but soon found this arrangement uncomfortable – and unsuccessful. She heard the crow call out again. In frustration, Naomi turned onto her stomach. She hugged her pillow and silently began to cry.

In the kitchen downstairs, Keiko and Sara were sitting together at the breakfast table, huddled over a pile of books. The younger woman's face was etched with worry; the older woman's face was a study in sympathy.

"Keiko-san, Naomi just isn't happy at all. She is becoming so withdrawn." Sara stared down at her hands. "I could tell she was really trying for the first few days. But now she doesn't say much. It's almost like she's given up. And I've got to start work next week. I won't be able to keep her company all day. She just seems so ... hopeless. It's really not like her at all." Sara looked up again at the older woman. "I don't know what to do."

Keiko put a consoling hand over her friend's. There was a long silence before she spoke. "I am not sure there is anything you can do, Sara-san. Apart from returning to Canada. Or sending Naomi home alone ..."

"That is not an alternative. We aren't going home," Sara answered firmly. She held on to Keiko's hand. "I'm so grateful that I have you here, Keiko-san. Without you, I don't know what we'd do. I had a chance, and I took it. It was a giant leap, but I – we – are here now and we're going to make it work."

Keiko patted the young woman's hand and rose from the table. She returned moments later with a tea pot and two cups on a tray. As she poured the green tea, Keiko looked over at Sara and smiled. "Well, we'll have to make it work, then. But give her time, Sara-san. It's a big step. Think of it."

"Oh, I know," Sara replied as she took the teacup in both hands. "Believe me, I have put myself in her position. I honestly don't know if I would have been able to handle all this very well myself."

Keiko sat down again and took a sip from her teacup. "Maybe we should help her find some – focus," she said, searching for the right word.

"You mean about school, and her lessons? Things to do?" Sara asked.

"Yes, something like that. She needs to think about other things. She probably sees the year ahead as one long and lonely road."

"Yes, you're right. She doesn't need to start her home schooling until September, but it wouldn't do any harm to give her the schoolbooks now, as well as all the books about Japan I bought for her yesterday. It will give her some time to think about it. She's always been a good student. I'm just worried that she seems so – unmotivated."

Keiko added, "I'm sure she would be interested in learning about traditional Japanese culture; the sports, music and art. There really is so much to learn. I'm excited about it myself."

"And I'll ask that girl you introduced us to the other day at the grocery store – Midori – to join us this evening when we go to the neighbourhood *Obon* Festival," Sara said. She thought for a moment before continuing, "Naomi needs to make some friends. She's spending too much time with her Walkman, and writing letters and e-mailing her friends back home – " Sara was about to say more when Naomi entered the room.

"*Ohayo*," Keiko and Sara said in unison as Naomi walked over to the kitchen cupboard and took out a teacup. She went to the refrigerator and poured herself some orange juice.

"*Ohayo*," Naomi replied, flashing a glum look in Keiko's direction as she sat down at the table. Then she focused her red-rimmed eyes on her mother. "I don't think there's anything wrong with keeping in touch with my friends," she said quietly, trying hard to control the anger in her voice. Despite her feelings, she had remembered something her mother had told her a long time ago; that people in Japan do not often show their anger to others. Naomi felt so full of anger at that moment, it surprised her. She wasn't sure she could keep it all inside her.

Sara's face flushed. She smiled anxiously at Naomi and said, "Keiko-san and I know you must be feeling very lonely. Maybe bored as well. We want you to know that we understand and want to help you. Now, you don't have to start your home schooling until Septem – "

Naomi looked up. *So it's really happening! I'm really going to be here for a whole year!* The thought ricocheted in her mind. Hearing her mother mention the words "home schooling" had finally made the nightmare real. It was as if, until that moment, Naomi thought it all could have been a bad dream, that it was all going to end soon. Although Naomi knew she would be doing her schoolwork by correspondence – in fact it was her preference, rather than being left behind a year when she returned to Portage la Prairie – her mother was now telling her what she didn't want to believe: In September, she wasn't going to be heading off to school with her best friends Imee and Lois.

"I don't want to do that!" Naomi cried out at her mother. She felt her face crumple as she looked from her mother to Keiko. "I don't want to be here anymore. I want to go home!" she screamed and jerked herself out of her chair. Her half-empty teacup tipped over, spilling orange juice across the table. Mortified and embarrassed, Naomi shot a wide-eyed look at Keiko, turned, and fled up the stairs to the bedroom. She slammed the door, dived for her futon, and lay in a crumpled heap.

It was over half an hour before her mother gingerly entered the room, carrying the stack of books and some audio cassettes. Naomi could sense that her mother was standing over her, watching, as her head lay hidden under the pillows. Used tissues were scattered all around.

"Naomi," Sara's voice was little more than a whisper. After a few moments the woman repeated, "Naomi – please – let's talk. We need to talk. Naomi." Naomi could feel her mother get down on the futon beside her.

She made her mother wait a few minutes more before slowly raising herself on one elbow and looking at her. She saw her mother's sad and startled look. Naomi knew she looked awful, her eyes almost swollen shut. But she didn't care. She just wanted to go home.

"Naomi, please," her mother began. There was a desperate, pleading, tone in her voice that Naomi had never heard before, and it frightened her. She sat up, glancing at the books that her mother had spread out.

It looks like a lot of work, whatever it is, Naomi thought.

She reached for another tissue. "I want to go home. I can stay with Baba and Gigi and go back to my own school," she said. Naomi tried to control the tremor in her voice, but it just sounded mechanical.

Her mother's hands started to shake as they reached for a tissue. "No, Naomi. We're staying here – "

"YOU stay here! I'LL go back to MANITOBA!" Naomi's voice rose shrilly.

"Naomi. Stop," her mother hissed, her voice becoming stronger. "You don't yell in this house. And you do NOT disrespect Keiko-san like that. She is my dear friend, and I'm grateful for her support. I don't know where we'd be if it weren't for her generosity."

Naomi shot her mother a sneer and blew her nose.

Sara sat up, startled by her daughter's rude behaviour. "Naomi. Things were okay last week. You seemed interested in everything around you. It reminded me of how I felt when I first came to Japan." She sighed, her shoulders drooping. "I should have known things were not going to be so easy. I know I'm asking a lot of you. Do you think I wanted things to turn out this way, Naomi? Do you? I'm thirty-five years old – I have a twelve-year-old daughter. Your father rarely keeps in touch. No husband," Sara said as she reached for another tissue and dabbed at her eyes. "No home of our home. I lost my job." She rested her hands in her lap and looked down at them for a long time before continuing, "I'm doing my best, Naomi, although you might not think so. There comes a time when you just have to make it work, wherever you find yourself."

"I want to go home!" Naomi repeated. She could feel herself slipping out of control, but she didn't care. "I hate this place!" she cried out. "I don't understand anything – it's all in Japanese. There's nothing good on TV –"

"Well, that's a good thing," her mother cut in, sarcastically.

"You don't understand. You never asked me if I wanted to do this," Naomi wailed. "It was just about you – what you wanted. What about ME?"

"I had no choice, Naomi. Don't you see that?"

"Yes you did. We could have stayed with Baba and Gigi. They wanted us to," Naomi stated defiantly.

Sara paused for a moment before speaking. "Yes, Naomi. We could have stayed with my mom and dad. But then what? For how long, Naomi?" she tenderly brushed away a strand of Naomi's hair, stuck by tears to her daughter's face. "Just ... just trust me, Naomi. It doesn't have to be as bad as it seems to you right now, with a little attitude adjustment. Try to understand, Naomi, I'm doing the best I can." She fell silent. Naomi had never seen her mother look so defeated. Not even when they were all going through the divorce.

She watched in silence as her mother took a few deep breaths and rose from the futon. At the door, she turned to face her daughter once more, "Please think about what I said. I know this isn't easy for you, but I love you, so we're going to stick together. Maybe we'll go home for Christmas, or something, if we can afford it. When you're ready, please come down. We'll go to the *Obon* Festival with Keiko-san and that nice girl, Midori, who lives down the street."

Then, as an afterthought, she added, "Sometimes, when you take a leap into the unknown, you may discover that you've landed in a good place – and on your feet as well. I have to believe that, Naomi. I hope you will, too." With that, she turned and walked out the door, closing it behind her.

Naomi sat rigidly on her futon, staring at the door. It seemed as if her ears were ringing. All she could think about was how defeated her mother had looked. How completely sad. Slowly, she began to understand that moving to Japan had not been an easy decision for her mother to make. *I'm doing the best I can. Attitude adjustment.* Naomi played these words over and over in her mind.

Tentatively, she reached for one of the books laying on her mother's futon: *Remembering the Kanji.* Naomi flipped through it, admiring the exotic-looking calligraphy. It was a book on how to write the Chinese symbols used in the Japanese written language. Naomi had to admit it looked interesting. She reached for another book: *An Introduction to Haiku.* Naomi liked haiku, and poetry in general. She had learned about the special Japanese form of poetry in English class last year. Naomi opened the book and her eyes fell upon a haiku poem by somebody called Basho:

> *in early autumn*
> *rice fields and ocean*
> *one green*

Intrigued, she reached for another book, with a large brightly coloured cover: *Crow Boy.* Naomi smirked, thinking of the morning's altercation with the crow, as she opened the book to page one. It was a beautifully illustrated book for young children, written in both English and the easy-to-read Japanese *hiragana* phonetic alphabet. It was not a long story, and Naomi spent a couple of minutes reading the first few pages before she found herself drawn to the rest of the books on her mother's bed: *Hiragana and Katakana for Dummies; Totto-chan – The Little Girl at the Window; Sadako and The Thousand Paper Cranes; The Story of Momo-Taro and Other Japanese Folk Tales.*

Naomi flipped through them all. "Well, it's going to be interesting reading," she decided grudgingly. She loved books. She reached for *Crow Boy* again, settled back against the pillows, and read the story of the funny little schoolboy right through to the end.

The Obon Festival

The doorbell rang as Naomi was clearing the supper dishes. "Naomi-chan, can you get that, please? It must be Midori," her mother said.

Naomi looked over at her mother who was standing at the sink, washing the dishes. She rolled her eyes. *Now mom's calling me "Naomi-chan," too*, she thought, annoyed.

Nervously, Naomi went to the front door. What was she supposed to say? Did Midori speak any English – more than just hello and thank you? She took a deep breath and opened the door. Before her stood a small girl in a flowered dress and shiny white shoes. Her hair was smooth and straight and jet-black. It was done up in two short pigtails, with pink bows on each side of her head. Naomi noticed she was gripping a small shiny white purse in one hand, and a box wrapped with ribbon in the other. *She looks younger than me*, Naomi decided, *and a little nervous herself.* Speechless, the little girl held out the gift box in front of her with both hands. The shiny white purse fell to the ground.

"Ah," the girl said, and bent to pick it up, while struggling to hold up the gift box in front of her. At the same time, Naomi also bent down to retrieve the girl's funny-looking purse. Their heads almost collided and both girls reared back, embarrassed.

"Uh – sorry," Naomi mumbled.

"*Ah – sumimasen*," Midori squeaked.

Keiko came to the door and took the gift box from the girl with a smile. They exchanged greetings in Japanese. Looking at the box in her hands, and then to Naomi, Keiko explained, "This is *omiyage* – a Japanese custom. We often bring a gift – usually food – when we visit someone at home." Midori nodded eagerly to Naomi as Keiko spoke, and performed a nervous little bow.

"*O jama shimasu*," Midori said, bowing nervously again as she stepped into the house and removed her shoes.

Keiko laughed at the confused look on Naomi's face. "Midori has very good manners. We say *O jama shimasu* when we enter someone's home. It means something like, 'I am being rude.' It is very polite."

Midori was smiling and nodding at Keiko and Naomi all the while. *She's bizarre*, Naomi thought, as she watched the smiling, nodding, very polite little girl. Naomi wondered how much the girl had really understood.

Keiko took a pair of flowered guest slippers from a shelf beside the door, and placed them in front of Midori's little feet. Midori put the slippers on and followed Naomi and Keiko down the pine-covered hallway as far as the living room. There, they removed their slippers and walked into the *tatami*-covered room. Keiko motioned for the girls to sit down on the *tatami* mats, at a low polished wooden table. Naomi's mother came in with a pitcher of lemonade and some forks, glasses, and plates on a tray. Keiko opened the gift box to reveal four pieces of cake. Each piece was different: marble cheesecake, strawberry shortcake, pound cake and a brownie.

"Mmmm. *Oishiso*. They look delicious," Sara said in both English and Japanese. "*Midori-chan*, which is your favourite?"

"Strawberry shortcake is my favourite cake," Midori answered in her sweet-sounding voice. Naomi's ears pricked up at the familiar words, spoken with the unfamiliar Japanese accent.

Sara smiled warmly at the girl. "Your English is very good."

Midori smiled eagerly. "I like English," she replied, and turned to Naomi. "Please teach me English better."

Naomi looked at the girl, and then at Keiko and her mother, not knowing how to respond. She didn't want to sound rude to this well-mannered girl. "Okay. Please teach me Japanese."

Midori's eyes opened wide and she brought her hands together in an excited little clap. "Okay! You teach me – I teach you!"

Naomi thought the girl was acting a little too excited about language lessons. "Okay," she replied simply, then found herself stifling a giggle as Midori once again eagerly clapped her hands.

Sara passed out the cakes and Keiko poured glasses of lemonade for the girls. The conversation fell into a comfortable mix of easy English and Japanese.

"*Nan sai desu ka?* How old are you?" Naomi's mother asked.

Midori held up the fingers on both her hands and then two fingers on her right hand. "I'm twelve years old," she announced, and looked over at Naomi, expectantly.

"I'm twelve," Naomi replied and then, hesitantly: "*Jiu-ni sai.*"

"*Sugoi!*" said Midori, wide-eyed.

Midori looked excited to hear such simple news. Naomi wondered why. *What's she so excited about?* But deep inside, Naomi knew she wanted to be happy like that, too. She wanted to be happy about little things, like meeting a girl the same age as yourself, like she used to be. Back home.

"*Ja. Ikimashooka?* Shall we go?" Keiko asked. "The *Obon* festivities have started at our neighbourhood park."

"Can't wait, Keiko-san. Naomi will love it," replied Sara. "Let me just clear these plates. Naomi, why don't you run upstairs and get your camera – take Midori with you."

Midori looked around the bedroom with undisguised interest as Naomi stood, trying to remember where she had put her camera.

"Who are they?"

Naomi turned around, and saw Midori pointing to a photograph on her desk; the one of herself, with her friends Imee and Lois. They were standing in a large, "U-pick" strawberry field, each proudly holding up a large bucket of berries. Naomi smiled and walked over to Midori.

"This is Imee. This is Lois. They are my friends," Naomi explained happily, pointing to each girl as she spoke. She smiled fondly at the photograph, remembering the day it was taken, and realized that it was not all that long ago. She liked the picture; if you looked closely, you could see that all three girls had red streaks over their mouths. That day they'd eaten almost as many strawberries as they had put into their buckets. Then Baba had made a bunch of delicious strawberry pies ...

"Did you eat many strawberries?" asked Midori, pointing to the girls' faces. Naomi laughed, impressed that she had noticed.

"Naomi," Sara called out from downstairs.

Naomi pulled her camera out from her rucksack. "Coming," she replied. Midori carefully returned the photo to its place and the two girls headed downstairs.

They headed out the door in the direction of the playground. In the distance, they could hear the sounds of Japanese music and of children having fun. The park was crowded. Multicoloured Japanese lanterns had been strung in a wide circle and glowed invitingly in the darkness. People were strolling alongside the various food and game stalls. Naomi grimaced, and sniffed tentatively at the strange, exotic mix of smells in the air. Loud music began to play. Recognizing a familiar tune, Midori excitedly grabbed Naomi's arm and pulled her through the crowd towards the circle of coloured lights. They pulled up to a wide open space, bordered by a circle of people, lined up back to front. They were all stepping and waving their arms in unison.

It's like line-dancing, Naomi thought, intrigued.

"Japanese *Bon* dance," Midori explained, and, with her hand still firmly gripping Naomi's arm, pulled her into the line of dancers. People turned to look and smile at Midori and Naomi, making room for the two girls. Midori fell into step immediately with the rest of the group, stepping forwards and then back, waving her arms gracefully over her shoulder.

In line behind her, Naomi fumbled as she tried to follow Midori's graceful movements. She looked up and saw her mother and Keiko in the crowd watching her. Keiko was smiling encouragingly as her mother suppressed a giggle. "What am I doing?" Naomi muttered under her breath, and then, surprising herself, she laughed out loud. She felt silly, but everyone was having such a good time. Midori turned to see how Naomi was doing and smiled at her progress. After several minutes, Naomi had almost mastered the steps. She looked around at the circle of dancers and could see several people watching her, nodding and smiling approvingly.

At the other side of the circle, Naomi saw Keiko and her mother join the line, and laughed in spite of herself as her mother struggled to master the steps just as she herself had done. She could hear Midori laughing, too. All too soon, the music ended and the line dispersed. Midori and Naomi ran into the centre of the circle to meet up with Keiko and Sara. All of them were flushed with excitement.

"*Jozu*. You are good," Keiko said. "You are a fast learner, Naomi-chan."

"Isn't that true," Midori added in Japanese.

They continued to wander through the crowd. Naomi noticed that children were holding toys and prizes of all kinds: balloons and face masks, even small plastic bags containing goldfish swimming in water. Midori and Naomi approached a vendor who appeared to be selling something popular. Naomi craned her neck and saw rows of large white, doughy-looking balls in clear plastic boxes. She took a closer look and could see something inside, underneath the translucent layer of white dough. Naomi guessed it was something sweet. *It almost looks like Baba's plum perogies*, Naomi thought.

"*Anko mochi*," Midori said, and pointed to the food. "Do you like *mochi*?"

"I don't know," Naomi replied. She thrust a bill at the vendor, and pointed to a box of six. Naomi and Midori found some room at a picnic table and opened the box, each helping themselves to a piece. Naomi bit into the soft, chewy white dough. She was disappointed; it was a strange, gluey texture, almost like it was raw. Inside, the filling was red and lumpy and dry. It was almost too sweet. She wondered what it was.

"*Mame*."

Naomi looked up. An old man was sitting at their table, with his little granddaughter. They were both looking at her. He pointed to the *anko mochi* in her hand. "*Mame*," he repeated.

Naomi looked at Midori, who nodded in agreement. "*Mame*," Midori said, then added, "I don't know – in English." Then she had an idea. She grabbed a small stick that lay on the ground nearby and drew a picture in the sandy pathway next to the table. Naomi could see that she was drawing a picture of a small seed with a stem and two leaves. For some reason, it reminded her of growing bean plants in school.

"Bean?" she asked. Midori shrugged, not sure, herself.

"Beee!" the little granddaughter cried out merrily, reaching for the stick that Midori was holding.

They all laughed at the clever little girl. Naomi shrugged, then pointed to the sweet snack she was holding. "*Oishii*," she said, hoping that she was being polite enough.

The man and his little granddaughter nodded. The little girl smiled. "*Oishii*," she said and held out her hands expectantly. The grandfather gently lowered the girl's hands in rebuke.

Naomi held out the box to the girl. "*Dozo*," she said, as the girl eagerly took one of the *mochi* in her hands and bit into it. Naomi held the box to the older man, who bowed as he gingerly took one of the three remaining *anko mochi*.

Then, from somewhere behind her, Naomi heard a pop-pop-pop sound. "*Hanabi*," Midori exclaimed excitedly, and stood up, pointing at the sky.

"That must mean fireworks," Naomi deduced, and stood to get a better view. She thought the fireworks were loud and not very big, but she could see that the crowd was enjoying it nonetheless. Within a few minutes the fireworks display had ended. Midori bowed to the older man, who bowed slightly from where he sat. Naomi watched and followed Midori's actions. The man smiled and bowed again. His granddaughter clapped her hands and said something in Japanese. Both Midori and the old man laughed at the little girl.

"She likes your hair. Like ... gold," Midori explained to Naomi.

Naomi looked around and realized that she was the only person with blonde hair in the whole park. She grabbed a handful of her hair and shook it at the girl. "Bye-bye," Naomi said and smiled, then turned to follow Midori into the crowd to find Keiko and her mother.

On the way home, Keiko explained the meaning of the *Obon* Festival. "It's a festival to celebrate our ancestors," she began. "All over Japan, people return to their home towns to worship at the graves of their loved ones. And," she added, "It's a chance to have a little fun, too."

They paused in front of Midori's house. After bowing and exchanging a few words with Keiko in Japanese, Midori turned to Naomi and her mother. "Bye-bye. See you again."

"See you again, Midori," Sara replied.

They watched as Midori walked up the path to her home. A woman opened the door and waved at them as Midori entered. Keiko bowed in the darkness and called out a cheerful greeting.

"Midori's mother and father are a lovely couple. They lived in the United States for three years," Keiko explained as they continued their walk home. "Mr. Takenaka is the principal of Pippu Elementary School. Right now, he is in Sapporo, visiting with his own mother and father."

When they arrived home, Naomi wrote another long e-mail to Lois and a letter to Baba and Gigi, and then went to bed. It had been a good day, after all. In the darkness, she let a smile creep across her face. But as soon as she did so, the now-familiar ache in her chest came back with a vengeance, and Naomi's smile vanished. *I'm alone in Japan*, she thought, *and that's nothing to smile about.*

Discovering the Snow Museum

It was a bright September day, and Naomi decided she deserved a break from her science book. She had been doing home-schooling for two weeks now. In that time, she had discovered that concentrating on something, like her studies, had a way of taking her mind off of missing Manitoba. She had jumped into her studies with fervour, because it made her feel connected to her friends back home. *Gotta keep up with everyone back home*, Naomi would say to herself over and over. She e-mailed and wrote letters often, and eagerly awaited the postman's arrival every day. She relished every letter from Imee and Lois and Baba and Gigi and yet found herself wishing for more. Naomi found herself wondering if Imee and Lois would forget about her. Maybe Billy would forget her, too. Naomi felt a need to stay in touch with Manitoba as much as she could. "I don't want everyone to forget me – to make friends without me!" she cried out, when her mother said she should do something other than send letters home. Naomi got angry when her mother suggested she was spending too much time in her room.

But looking out her bedroom window, Naomi felt that she just couldn't let the day pass without enjoying the freshness outside. Calling to Keiko to let her know where she was going, Naomi laced up her running shoes and headed out towards the nearby park, where the

Obon Festival had been held weeks before. As she got closer, she could hear the sounds of young children playing. *Funny how it sounds just like any playground in Portage la Prairie*, she thought to herself. She turned the corner, which opened onto a broad expanse of earth, rimmed with grass and trees. Inside the earthen square were swings, slides, and see-saws. Children were crawling all over them, making the usual playground din. Naomi smiled as she surveyed all the mothers sitting on benches around the playground area. She walked over, sat down, and smiled as children began, one by one, to notice her.

"*Gaijin! Gaijin da!*" shouted one little boy as he extended a pudgy finger in Naomi's direction and ran towards his mother.

"*Gaijin! Gaijin!*" Almost all the little children began to laugh and others pointed. Naomi sat forward in her seat, not knowing what to do. She had only just sat down and didn't want to leave yet. She began to feel self-conscious and uncomfortable; embarrassed and annoyed by the finger-pointing. Scolding mothers whispered into their children's ears. A group of little girls wanted to make friends, and were slowly inching their way towards Naomi, but she didn't notice.

She got up and jogged away, back towards the safe refuge of Keiko's home. Dejected, she opened the front door and went up to her room. She stared out the window at the hills and felt sorry for herself. She was trapped. There was nothing she could do.

Slowly, feelings of sadness gave way to anger. Those mean little boys were the last straw! Naomi knew that word: *gaijin*. "That's not a nice thing to say. It means 'outsider,'" Naomi muttered under her breath. "They think I'm an alien – or worse." She had never felt so outside of things. All alone in this country. Her mother working all day. Going to school all by herself in her little room. All she wanted to do was go home. *Go home!*

Restless, Naomi got up and stood at the window. The cicadas' shrill buzzing seemed to grow into a deafening crescendo about her ears and the bedroom felt hot and stuffy. She wanted so much to be with Imee and Lois that her stomach began to tie into a knot of fear. Naomi bolted down the stairs and out of the house. The front door slammed behind her as she jumped onto her bicycle. She rode through the front gate as Keiko watched, surprised, from the front window.

Naomi began pedalling as fast as she could, barely able to see through her tear-filled eyes. She pedalled far down the street even before she knew where she wanted to go. As she picked up speed and the crisp autumn wind whipped her cheeks, Naomi began to feel she was once again free. A smile began to play across the girl's face and she sped up. She knew where she wanted to go. Anywhere but here.

She rode her bicycle far along the river, past a group of high school boys, down an embankment and up a steep and narrow road. When she no longer had the strength to pedal, she got off her bike and pushed it up the hill. She could feel her anger and sadness diminish through the physical effort, and was grateful for it. Then, through the tops of the pine trees, she saw the strangest thing. It was a large silver snowflake.

Naomi continued pushing her bicycle up the road, trying not to let the snowflake out of her sight. As she rounded a curve in the narrow road, the snowflake came into full view. It was atop one of the oddest and most beautiful buildings she had ever seen. "This can't be real," she whispered. "What is it?" The walls were a brilliant white in the afternoon sun, and there were several cupolas with rounded roofs painted a deep blue. Transparent blue and white stained-glass windows shimmered on all the walls. And, at the highest point, the lone silver snowflake glinted in the sun.

Looks just like those Ukrainian onion-dome churches all over Manitoba, Naomi thought, mesmerized. Yet this church was a sparkling white and blue. And instead of a cross at the top of the onion dome, there was that amazing silver snowflake! In some strange way, the building reminded Naomi of home, of the place she needed to be. She parked her bicycle and walked up the stairs to the door. Naomi tried her best to read the sign, written in the *katakana* phonetic alphabet. She sounded out the characters: *su-no myu-ji-a-mu*. Snow Museum!

What kind of place is a Snow Museum? Naomi asked herself with amazement as she entered the sparkling building. Inside, the deep blue sky painted across the ceiling was like the deepest blue velvet, an ocean of stars. Naomi walked the sparkling corridors of what looked like an art gallery, admiring the paintings, each one with a winter theme. She came upon room after room of delights. There was a library, filled with nothing but books about snow, winter, and Christmas. Naomi wandered into a room of computers which taught all about snow crystals and wild storms, penguins, and polar bears.

She was amazed to discover that the video footage about polar bears was from Churchill, Manitoba! She wandered into a narrow crystal corridor, with a shiny royal-blue tile floor. On each side of the darkened hallway, stalactites of ice shimmered in the light behind tall glass windows. Naomi gasped, and shivered in the cold. "Mom's not going to believe this," she whispered.

The crystal corridor opened up into a large room. It was obviously a concert hall of some kind. There were about one hundred seats and a stage with heavy ice-blue satin curtains all around the room. On the stage was one lonely black chair, and a girl, holding a violin, talking to a man wearing oversized earphones. Naomi stepped back, half-hidden in the folds of the curtain, and watched as the girl took her seat on the stage and began to play. Naomi thought the music sounded sad, and she quietly took a seat at the back of the crystal hall, letting her feelings flow with the sad and lonely strains of the violin.

Making Friends

Naomi left the Snow Museum and walked over to a park bench under some nearby trees. Still amazed by what she had just seen, she sat and looked up at the awesome church-like building. Naomi dreaded having to go back to Pippu-cho. She thought about her new home. It had been her home for less than two months. There was so much longer to go before she could go home to Manitoba.

Think happy thoughts, she told herself, as she knew Baba would tell her. She listed in her mind all the things that made her happy about this place. The Snow Museum was an amazing find! *That's at the top of my list now,* she thought. But her mind was crowded out by all the things that made her sad and lonely. She couldn't help it.

I'm lonely, Naomi admitted to herself. *Seeing neat new things, like this Snow Museum, can't change that. I have nobody to share them with. I miss Lois and Imee, Baba and Gigi. I miss my dog. I miss riding my bicycle down Main Street. I miss my school. I'm alone every day.* Naomi let these thoughts spin around in her mind, and was soon feeling miserable. Nine long months to go. She thought again about the little boys in the park and the word they called her: *gaijin.*

As she continued to gaze into the distance, her eye was caught by three small figures approaching the museum on bicycles. Naomi could see that it was three girls in school uniforms. One girl waved in her direction.

Naomi sat up. Who could that be? Was it someone just coming to visit the Snow Museum? Then she recognized Midori. Naomi stood and started walking in their direction, trying to think of something in Japanese to say to them. Making conversation in a foreign language seemed so hard to do, even though she was almost always understood, in one way or another. Naomi sighed. All of a sudden she felt very tired.

The girls stopped their bicycles in front of her, and Midori introduced her two friends, Ai and Kiyoka. Ai, a big girl, asked, "*Daijobu desuka?* – Are you okay?"

Midori added in broken English, "We went to your house. Keiko-san said you are not happy. She said you take your bicycle but she doesn't know where you go."

Puzzled, Naomi asked, in the easiest English she could think of, "Why you come here – to the Snow Museum?"

Kiyoka, a tall and elegant girl with long hair tumbling down her back, jumped in, pulling out her little English dictionary and pointing to the word "ask." "We ask people. Where is the Canadian girl on bicycle? Do you see her? People say – 'On the side of the river.' Some high-school boys say ..." Kiyoka stopped, at a loss for words. She pointed off in the distance. "*Asoko* – Over there," she finished, smiling as if exhausted. Everyone laughed.

Ai added, tapping her head with her forefinger, "I think – Snow Museum?"

Naomi was amazed. Conflicting thoughts ran through her mind: *It's like everyone knows me here. It's amazing how these girls would know where to find me. But they don't talk to me – most of them – whenever I see someone my age at the store, or somewhere. Only Midori talks to me. What's wrong with me? I'm not weird. And those nasty little boys in the park – so mean!* Naomi's smile began to fade and Midori asked, "Why you are sad?"

"I miss my Canadian friends. I miss my school. *Sabishii*," Naomi replied. That word, *sabishii*, meant "lonely," and was one of the first words she had learned in Japanese. It was a feeling so strong she found it was something she had wanted to communicate right away to Keiko. She was glad to be able to express this feeling to these three girls. The three girls nodded their heads sympathetically.

"I hear *Gaijin! Gaijin!*" Naomi added, pointing her finger at the girls. Outsider. The idea that visitors can never really feel at home in

Japan felt so true to Naomi at this moment, and it was summed up by this one word.

Ai cut in indignantly, pointing as Naomi had done, "Who say *Gaijin! Gaijin!?*"

Naomi, suddenly a little embarrassed by Ai's obvious concern, mumbled, "Oh, little boys."

The girls smiled ruefully and Midori stepped forward to put her hand tentatively on Naomi's arm. "Don't worry – little boys, Naomi-chan," she said.

Kiyoka added, "That's right, don't worry." She placed her finger to her right temple, made a circular motion, and said, "Little boys. *Kurukuru-pa!*" The three girls began to laugh. Naomi stood smiling, waiting for an explanation.

Ai offered it. "Little boys! Crazy! *Kurukuru-pa!*" she said, making the same twirling motion with her finger at her temple. Again, the three girls broke down in peals of laughter. Naomi understood. Little boys were not be taken seriously. Deep down, she already knew this. Little children did not understand the consequences of their actions, if they were hurting people's feelings. This was true everywhere in the world. Naomi blushed. Didn't the adults of Pippu-cho always treat her with friendliness and kindness? She couldn't know everyone, of course. But Naomi began to realize that even if some people appeared afraid of her, or made fun of her or something – like those little children in the park – it was probably just shyness, or because it was something new to them. Naomi knew about that – it was something she tried to overcome every day here in Japan. And in Canada, too, sometimes.

Naomi chided herself. She knew she would have to make a greater effort to make friends, and to learn Japanese. She mustered up some of her beginner's Japanese and asked, "*Ima, doko ni ikimasu ka?* – Where are you going now?"

Ai replied in Japanese, "I'm hungry, let's go to a *ramen* shop."

Midori said, "*Ii kangae* – Good idea." Kiyoka nodded in agreement.

"Yeah! *Tabemashoo* – Let's eat," Naomi said and laughed as the four girls hopped on their bicycles and followed Ai in the direction of Pippu-cho. After ten minutes they stopped in front of a small restaurant with an orange-red awning. Naomi sounded out the word on the awning: *ramen.*

"*Ramen,*" she read slowly, "What's *ramen?*"

"*Ramen* is noodle soup. It is Chinese," Midori explained.

"*Oishii*. Num-num," Ai said, rubbing her stomach, and everyone laughed. It was clear to Naomi that Ai loved to eat. The four girls entered the *ramen* shop and took a booth in the corner. Midori grabbed the menu and placed it in front of Naomi beside her. She pointed to each item as she read from the menu, written partly in *katakana*, and partly in Chinese characters.

"Pork *ramen*, *miso ramen*, shrimp *ramen*," Midori read. Naomi repeated the menu along with her, resolving to remember everything. She pointed to the *miso* dish and said, "*Kore o tabetai* – I want to eat this."

The waitress came and the four girls ordered their meals. As they were waiting, Midori said quietly in Japanese, "Really, Naomi, don't worry, please."

Kiyoka added in Japanese, "Yes. You, Naomi, are a friend."

"Little boys. *Kurukuru-pa!*" Ai said again, and they laughed.

The laughter died down to silence. Kiyoka moved as if to say something, then stopped herself. The girls' eyes were on her. Kiyoka looked around the table at her friends. She hesitated for a moment, looked straight at Naomi, then spoke almost inaudibly in broken English, "*Toki-doki*. Sometimes," she began, "There are rude people. I live in Sapporo many years ago. People are rude to me in Sapporo."

Naomi looked at Kiyoka quizzically. She noticed Midori and Ai nodding knowingly. Ai put her hand on Kiyoka's arm. "*Naze?* – Why?" Naomi asked.

"I am Ainu," Kiyoka replied. "My grandmother is Ainu."

Naomi understood the word "Ainu." Keiko had told her about the indigenous race of people who lived in Japan, mainly in Hokkaido, long before the Japanese race had begun to inhabit the island.

"*Himitsu desu*," Kiyoka said.

Midori put her finger to her lips. "Secret," she said.

"Why?" Naomi asked, startled.

Midori replied, her eyes flashing, "Sometimes people are rude about Ainu. Sometimes people don't like Ainu."

Kiyoka looked across at her friend Midori and smiled slightly. Then she sighed resignedly and added, "But now, just a little. I don't worry, now."

Naomi felt honoured that Kiyoka chose to tell her this secret. It was so unfair! Kiyoka was no different from Midori or Ai – not at all!

But when Naomi thought about the rudeness of the little boys in the park today, she began to realize the kinds of things that Kiyoka might have had to deal with at her old school when she was very young.

Naomi wanted to be real friends with these three girls, who had taken the trouble to find her at the Snow Museum.

"I went to the Ainu museum in Asahikawa a long time ago. It was very interesting," Midori said.

"I'd like to go to the Ainu museum," Naomi said.

Kiyoka's face brightened. "Let's go. Next week. *Suiyobi.*"

Naomi counted her fingers to remind herself what day of the week *Suiyobi* was: Wednesday. That was today, the day that students had only a half-day of school. She remembered how shocked she was when Keiko told her students went to school on Saturday mornings! She was only mildly relieved to hear, then, that Wednesdays were half-days. Naomi nodded to Kiyoka in agreement. The waitress brought over four enormous ceramic bowls heaped with noodles in a steaming broth, and the table was once again silent as the four young girls began to eat. The girls commented approvingly on Naomi's dexterity with her chopsticks.

Naomi demurely brushed aside their compliments in the Japanese style that Keiko had told her about. In Japan, it is considered good manners to ignore compliments. Ai, Midori and Kiyoka looked at each other and smiled knowingly. It was not uncommon for young people to know how to accept a compliment in the Western way. Their new Canadian friend was quickly becoming Japanese!

Kiyoka asked, "You like the Snow Museum?"

Naomi had almost forgotten about the place, as incredible as it was. "It's amazing! We don't have a Snow Museum in Manitoba," she replied, looking up from her bowl of *ramen.*

"Do you have snow in winter?" asked Midori.

Naomi laughed, "Lots of snow. It's very cold in the winter in Manitoba." She thought of the prospect of not having a snowy winter, and was glad that she would be going home for Christmas. "I miss the snow," she said in Japanese.

"No problem. We have a lot of snow in Pippu-cho," Midori said.

Surprised, Naomi put down her chopsticks. "You do?"

"*Mochiron!* – Of course!" Ai said, and the others laughed.

"Hokkaido and Asahikawa are famous for skiing," Midori added.

Naomi was confused, "Why do you need a museum, then, if you have snow every winter?"

The three girls sat back and laughed at Naomi, who began to laugh at herself, too. "Don't worry, Naomi. Lots of snow," chuckled Midori, as she returned her attention to the last of her noodles in the big bowl of broth.

"What time is it?" asked Ai

Kiyoka replied, "Oh! Eight o'clock."

Midori's eyes opened wide, "Yikes! It's late!"

The girls paid for their *ramen* and rushed out to their bicycles. Ai said a quick "Bye-bye" and raced off down the levy on her bike. Midori, Kiyoka and Naomi, who lived closer together, took a more leisurely pace as they biked along the river. As the rose-coloured sunset deepened to fuchsia, a bracing wind whipped again at Naomi's cheeks.

When they approached their neighbourhood, Kiyoka suddenly cried out, stopping her bicycle to point to the sky.

"*Ii, ne?* – Great, isn't it?"

Naomi looked up at the sky, which had now darkened to the colour of plums. And the setting sun, no longer visible behind the hills, was still illuminating the underside of a fleet of fluffy cumulous clouds, spread across the evening sky.

Kiyoka looked from the clouds to Naomi, and asked in Japanese, "What is the name of that colour, in English?"

Naomi opened her mouth, and was surprised to find that she had no reply. She couldn't think of a single English word to describe the colour of those clouds. She looked at Kiyoka, at a loss for words.

Kiyoka understood Naomi's dilemma. She threw her head back and laughed, "I don't know either, in Japanese. Bye-bye, Naomi. Bye-bye, Midori."

Naomi and Midori waved as Kiyoka rode down from the levy and onto the street. Then they raced home. Naomi couldn't wait to tell her mother and Keiko all of it – and everyone back home, too. All about her new friends, the *ramen* shop, and the amazing Snow Museum.

セ

Learning to Spell

"Naomi," Keiko began, "You've been in Japan for more than a month now. Would you like to try something a little more challenging?"

Naomi and Keiko were sitting on the second-floor balcony of Keiko's home, having their usual weekly lesson in Japanese culture.

"Good idea, Keiko-san," Naomi replied as she buttoned up her sweater. "I need help learning how to read and write in Japanese. I'm tired of going places and not being able to read the signs."

Keiko smiled warmly. "Learning any language is quite a challenge. So, what have you discovered since you've come here?"

"I know that the Japanese written language has many different kinds of alphabets, sort of." Naomi shuffled some of the books and papers on the table in front of her, and pointed to the pages in her book, *Crow Boy.* "This is *hiragana* – the Japanese phonetic alphabet. It's used in children's books, because it's easier to learn to read." Then Naomi reached for the morning Japanese newspaper and scanned the pages. She pointed at a word and said, "This is *katakana* – the Japanese phonetic alphabet that is used for foreign loan words."

Keiko nodded. "That's right – we also use *katakana* in things like advertising, too. It's very – 'catchy,'" she said, searching for the right word.

"There's also *romaji* – which means "Roman letters." It's a way of translating Japanese words into English, for people like me who can't read Japanese yet." Naomi grinned, and added, "I know *romaji* pretty well, because that's how I look up in my pocket dictionary all the Japanese words I hear." She then pointed to the front page of the newspaper and waved her hand across it, grimacing. "And most of this is *kanji*, the Chinese characters that are used in everyday written Japanese."

"That's right," Keiko confirmed. "But in Japanese writing, there is always a mix of the *kanji* with the *hiragana* and *katakana*. That is what makes the Japanese language different from Chinese – at least in writing. The two languages sound totally different, too, of course."

Naomi nodded. "I know that *kanji* is not a phonetic system. Each character is like a little picture; they each have meaning. There are thousands of them." She looked up at Keiko. "And not only that, but each one can be pronounced in different ways, depending on if they are written alone, or combined with other *kanji*." Naomi looked at the piles of pages in front of her and was overwhelmed. "What am I going to do? I can't read any of this," she said.

Keiko smiled sympathetically at Naomi's glum expression, "Yes, you're right, Naomi-chan. There are thousands of *kanji* in the Japanese written language. But, to be able to read the newspaper, you only need to know about two thousand. All children are taught these two thousand *kanji* characters before they graduate from high school."

"But how can you remember them all?" Naomi asked, scanning the front page of the paper with a look of awe.

"It's not so bad. Children start learning them right from grade one. It is all planned by the department of education in Tokyo. In grade one, for example, students will learn seventy-six *kanji*. In grade two, they will learn one-hundred and forty-five, and so on. Some of them are quite easy to remember because they often look like the meaning they represent." Keiko reached for a paper and a pen. She wrote two characters: 日 本

and pointed to the first one. "This is a picture of a sun. It can be pronounced *nichi, hi,* or *bi,* depending on the combination." Pointing to the character beside it, she said, "This is the symbol for 'book.' Book is usually pronounced *hon*. It can also mean 'origin' or 'foundation.'

Naomi was excited. "I didn't know that! I thought those two symbols together meant 'Japan.' It's the only thing I thought I knew. It's everywhere."

Keiko nodded, equally excited, "But you're right, Naomi-chan. This says *Ni-hon*: that is how we pronounce the word 'Japan.' So you can see the meaning of the name of our country, just by looking at the *kanji*. Japan means 'Origin of the sun.'"

"The Japanese flag is a big red circle – that's the sun, too," Naomi added. Then she asked excitedly, "How do you write 'Canada' in Japanese?"

"We can write 'Canada' in *katakana*, because it is a foreign loan word, like this," Keiko wrote:

カ ナ ダ

on the paper. "This way, it is pronounced ka-na-da. But we can also write it using kanji, like this," Keiko wrote:

加 国

on the paper.

"What does it mean?" Naomi asked eagerly.

Keiko pointed to the second symbol and said, "This is the symbol for 'country.' By itself, we pronounce it *kuni*. But when it is combined with another *kanji*, we can pronounce it *koku*." She pointed to the first character and said, "When combined with another *kanji*, this character is pronounced *ka*. When we write 'Canada' using *kanji*, we pronounce it *ka-koku* but I think most people write the word 'Canada' with katakana and say *ka-na-da*."

"But what does *ka* mean?" Naomi asked, puzzled.

"Well, I wish I could say something nice, or interesting, but it means simply 'to add.'" Keiko smiled as she saw Naomi's nose wrinkle up. "I think it was chosen for the sound alone, Naomi." She continued, writing:

on the paper. "England has a good name in *kanji*, though. This *kanji* was chosen for its 'eh' sound. It is the same *kanji* that we use to say *eigo*, as in the English language. England is pronounced *Ei-koku* and it means 'superior country.'"

Naomi pretended to be miffed, but then she grinned. "Please show me some more examples, Keiko-san."

50

Keiko thought for a moment, then wrote:

男

on the page. "This means 'man.' Can you see how the top part, the squares, remind one of a rice field?" she asked. Naomi nodded. "The bottom part means 'strength.' Can you imagine a man being strong in the fields?" Naomi was thinking about this image as Keiko wrote on the paper:

女

"This is the symbol for woman. Can you imagine a woman holding a baby in her arms?"

Naomi studied the symbol. If she turned her head and – with a bit of imagination, she could indeed. "I think I'll be able to remember which bathroom is which now, when I go in restaurants," she joked.

Keiko wrote:

木

on the paper. "This is 'tree:' Pronounced *ki* by itself. And this," she said, drawing the same symbol for tree, but this time with a box around it:

困

"means 'to be troubled' – *komaru*."

"This *kanji* stuff is pretty interesting. I suppose I'd feel troubled if I was a tree stuck inside a box with no room to grow."

"Exactly," Keiko said, and then wrote:

林

on the page. "Now look at this. Here I have drawn two trees growing together. "This means 'forest' – *hayashi*."

Naomi's eyebrows shot up. That was very clever. She watched as Keiko drew another tree symbol above the first two:

森

"This means 'woods' – *mori*." Then Keiko wrote the kanji for forest again, next to the *kanji* for woods.

"When you put these two *kanji* together, we pronounce it *shinrin*. What do you think it means, Naomi?"

"I think it means a pretty big bunch of trees!" replied Naomi, laughing.

"You're absolutely right, Naomi! We refer to the Amazon rainforest as a *shinrin*. And there isn't any bunch of trees bigger than that!"

Naomi was hooked. She promised herself she would learn as many characters as she could.

"So you see, Naomi. Sometimes you can picture the images and it will help you to remember. In fact, your mother gave you a book that shows you how to learn and remember *kanji* in that way. Have you looked at it yet?"

Naomi had to admit that it was under a pile of books, where she had left it weeks ago. She shook her head. "I've been reading the storybooks mom's given me, getting started with my home-schooling, and exploring. I've kind of been putting it off."

Keiko smiled and nodded. Finally, she spoke. "Well, I understand that you have been thinking about other things since you've been here. I'm glad to see that you've been doing your home-schooling. I know you are a bright girl, Naomi. Learning any new language isn't easy. Just go along at your own pace and enjoy it. The Japanese language is very different from English and French. Why don't we take a look at your book together?"

Naomi went upstairs and quickly returned with the book, a thick paperback. Keiko smiled at Naomi, opening the book to page one. "We'll just start at the beginning," she said.

"You mean, what I'm learning today is what little grade one students learn at school? Little five-year-olds?" Naomi asked, embarrassed.

Keiko could see the concern in her eyes, and tried to reassure her. "Yes, Naomi. But don't let that trouble you. We all have to start somewhere. It's nothing to be embarrassed about. You'll learn fast, I can tell." Naomi and Keiko spent some time studying the first few pages. Naomi wrote line after line in a large notebook, practising the correct way to write these complicated symbols. At the end of the class, Keiko handed her a small parcel wrapped in bright Japanese paper.

"What's this?" Naomi asked, smiling. But she was eagerly tearing at the wrapper before Keiko began to respond. Within seconds, Naomi was holding a small cloth-bound book. All the pages were blank. She looked up at Keiko quizzically.

"You can use it as a diary if you like. You might want to write about your life here in Japan, so you won't forget. Or, if you see a *kanji* you like, you can write it down in your book and it will help you to remember. You can use it to write whatever you want, really," Keiko explained.

Alone in her room later, Naomi stared at all the school books piled on her desk. She let out a big breath and ran her hand through her reddish-blonde hair. She fought down a wave a panic. *So much to learn. How can I do it?* she thought. *If I was back in Manitoba, things just wouldn't be as hard as all this.* Naomi looked longingly at the photograph of Imee and Lois on her desk. Then her eyes moved to the little cloth-bound notebook that Keiko had given her. She picked it up and held it in her hands for several minutes. Then, slowly, Naomi reached for a pen and began to write:

Dear Diary,

I'm lonely.
I miss everyone back home.
Today I started to learn how to spell. It's like having to start from scratch all over again. I am learning what grade one students learn. I'm glad that Imee and Lois don't know this.
It's pretty interesting, though.
I am. (I am troubled.) 木

Naomi's New Name

Naomi, Midori, Kiyoka and Ai were in the children's book section of Asahikawa's biggest department store. They had just spent a fascinating afternoon at the Ainu museum and folk village. Naomi realized that the Ainu people were, like the Ojibway and Sioux peoples of Manitoba, trying hard to keep alive their traditional way of life. Kiyoka had enjoyed showing Naomi, Midori and Ai the different displays and photos about how the Ainu people had lived in Hokkaido years ago. Kiyoka had many stories about her own grandmother, too, who had lived her young life very differently than the people in Japan did today.

"My stomach is rumbling," Ai joked. "Shall we go to Mister Donut?"

Naomi's ears pricked up when she heard the familar-sounding words. "Mister Donut?" she asked.

"Yes. Mister Donut coffee shop," Midori said. "I'm hungry, too."

Naomi nodded in agreement, then pointed to a display of children's elementary school posters. "Just a minute, please. I want to buy that," she said. She took one of the rolled-up posters to the cash register, while Ai, Kiyoka and Midori, standing behind her, shot each other amused glances.

Naomi recognized the Mister Donut sign from halfway down the block. *Looks interesting*, she thought to herself as they neared the shop.

She followed Midori in and was delighted at what she saw; a trendy-looking doughnut shop crowded with young people. American pop music was playing in the background, punctuated by a very American-sounding deejay. Lined on the wall behind the servers were at least 20 different kinds of doughnuts and other delicious-looking pastries. *I've got to show mom this place. It's almost like the Country Style Donut Shoppe back in Portage,* Naomi thought happily. She thought of her mother, who would never miss a chance to go for coffee and doughnuts back home. Naomi felt comforted by this familiar-looking place.

Midori, Kiyoka and Naomi each bought one doughnut and a drink. They laughed as Ai ordered two doughnuts to go with her iced tea. Carrying their trays, the girls carefully made their way between the crowded tables to an empty one near a group of older girls in high-school uniforms. All these girls wore big white knee socks that were pushed down around their ankles. Naomi noticed this and thought it looked rather sloppy. Ai gave Naomi a nudge, and shot a disapproving look at the older girls' baggy socks. Midori explained, "It is fashion now, in high school, to push socks down. The teachers say to them 'Don't do it. It is naughty.' But all the girls do it." She smiled and looked over at her friends, "In junior-high school, we don't do it."

Naomi looked from Midori, to the socks, then into the faces of the high-school girls. The older girls munched on their doughnuts and talked conspiratorially among themselves. A couple of them glanced coolly at Naomi, not quite concealing their interest in the foreign girl with the interesting red-blonde hair. Midori, as observant as always, noticed the look in their eyes. She whispered to Naomi, "They think you are an interesting *gaijin*. But," she smiled, "you come here with us. They know you are only a junior-high-school student." She paused, then added, "So you are not interesting." Naomi guffawed at her friend's surprising conclusion, causing all four of the high-school girls to look up and give Naomi and her friends another cool, appraising glance. Ai tossed her head at them, and motioned for her friends to take their seats. Ai then pointed at the poster sticking out of Naomi's rucksack. "Good idea," she said approvingly. Midori and Kiyoka nodded in agreement, smiling widely.

"I want to learn how to write Japanese," Naomi said weakly. She didn't know what else to say. How could she explain the fascination she'd felt when she and Keiko were having their first *kanji* lesson? But Naomi knew she was starting at the very beginning – like a young child – and felt embarrassed.

"Do you think *kanji* is interesting?" Kiyoka asked politely. Naomi nodded.

"Is it? Really?" Ai asked in disbelief. Then, yawning exaggeratedly, she added, "*Tsumaranai* – boring.""

Kiyoka took a pen and small notebook from her rucksack, and wrote two *kanji*:

"This is my name: *Kiyo-ka*. She flipped through her small pocket dictionary. "Meaning is 'pure' and 'fragrance,'" she explained, pronouncing the two words very carefully.

Ai grabbed the pen from Kiyoka and wrote one character on the paper:

愛

"One *kanji*," she said, and laughed her big laugh. "Easy – my name's meaning is 'love.'" Everyone giggled at that, Ai most of all. Then she pointed to herself. "Ai 'ravu' you," Ai finished jokingly, pointing at Naomi. The girls laughed at her comical pronunciation of the word "love."

Naomi realized that Ai had made a pun, that her friend's name and the word "I" sounded the same. She was thrilled: her friend had made a joke, at least partly in Japanese, and Naomi had understood it.

"What's the meaning of your name, Midori?" asked Naomi. All three girls giggled even louder at the question.

Midori looked embarrassed. "Midori means 'green,'" she said.

Naomi waited to hear the rest of it.

Midori giggled and lowered her eyes, "Only 'green.'"

They all laughed. After a pause, Kiyoka asked, "*Nay-oh-mee*. What is meaning?"

Naomi looked at the three girls, who were looking back at her expectantly. How could she explain to them there was no real meaning in the name "Naomi"? She shrugged. "Naomi has no meaning. It is just – well – sounds," she answered weakly, and then giggled at their crestfallen faces. Then Naomi thought of something Baba had told her a long time ago, and searched her memory to see if she could remember the whole story.

"Wait – Naomi has no meaning, like 'pure fragrance' or 'green' or 'love,'" she began. "But Naomi is a woman in the Bible. Do you know the Bible?" The three girls nodded as Naomi continued, "In the Bible, Naomi moved to a foreign land with her husband and two sons. But the men, they all died. Naomi wanted to go back to her homeland. She said to her two daughters-in-law" at this point, Naomi flipped through her pocket dictionary. "Daughter-in-law – ah, here it is. *Giri-no-musume.*" The girls nodded. "Anyway, Naomi said to them: 'You can stay here. You are young and can find new husbands.' One daughter-in-law stayed. But the other – her name was Ruth – said, 'No, I will go with you.' So Naomi and Ruth went back to Naomi's home and had a good life."

She stopped the story there. A long silence came over the group of girls, but Naomi wasn't aware of it. She was thinking about herself and her own mother, coming alone to Japan together. In some ways, their own story was very similar to the one she had just told, the story of Ruth and her mother-in-law. Midori put her hand lightly on Naomi's arm, and Naomi shook herself out of her reverie.

"Naomi is same spelling in *romaji*. Same in English." Midori said. She wrote the word "Naomi" on the piece of paper. "This is a Japanese name, too. Same in *romaji*, same in English. We say *Now-mee.*"

"Naomi is boy's name and girl's name. Naomi Uemura is a famous mountain climber. First Japanese man to climb Everest," Kiyoka added.

Naomi was thrilled. Her name was a Japanese name, too! It was pronounced a little differently, but it was spelled the same in its English translation. "No way! Mom never told me that!" she said excitedly. Then, quickly, she asked, "What is the meaning of *Now-mee?*"

The girls looked at each other before answering, talking back and forth in rapid Japanese. Naomi guessed that it was not a simple answer. Finally, Midori said, "You don't have a name in *kanji*. We will give you a name."

Midori, Kiyoka and Ai huddled over Kiyoka's little pocket dictionary. Naomi quietly sipped her lemonade, giggling as she watched the three girls excitedly try to take the small book out of each other's hands whenever they had an idea. They bantered on in rapid Japanese that Naomi couldn't understand, but she didn't mind. Instead, she smiled and watched her friends as they decided on a Japanese name for her. It took several minutes for the girls to come to an agreement, and Naomi watched with interest as Midori turned to a fresh page in Kiyoka's notebook and wrote two big characters that filled the page:

With a flourish, she ripped the page from its spiral binding and presented it to Naomi with a ceremonious bow. "This is your name: *Now-mee*. Most write *Now-mee*, the girl's name, like this. She pointed to the first character. "This means 'honesty.'"

Kiyoka pointed to the second character and said, "This means 'beauty.'"

"Naomi is – honesty and beauty," Ai repeated triumphantly, nodding at Midori and Kiyoka, and then across the table at Naomi.

Naomi looked across the table at the three girls, who were eagerly awaiting her reaction. She didn't know what to say.

The smile on Ai's face turned to a worried frown. "Is meaning 'honesty and beauty,' she said again, enunciating the two words carefully. "You not like meaning?"

"Oh, no – I mean, yes. Yes, I do. It's a beautiful meaning. Thank you," Naomi replied, much to the girls' relief. She took the paper in her hands and studied the two characters, trying to commit them to memory. She was flattered by the choice they had made. She looked up at her friends. "It's the best Japanese name I could have. I want to tell mom and Keiko-san."

The girls let out a relieved sigh. Ai picked up her big glass of iced tea and said, "*Now-mee* – honesty and beauty. *Kampai!*"

"*Kampai*," said Midori and Kiyoka as they clinked their glasses to Ai's.

"*Kampai*," Naomi chimed in. She raised her glass and joined her friends in a toast to her new Japanese name. Naomi felt proud and happy and glad to have these three girls as friends. It was strange to hear her name pronounced the Japanese way, but she liked it. Putting her glass down on the table, she announced, "From now on, please call me *Now-mee*."

Ai clapped Naomi on the back and raised her glass again. "*Kampai, Now-mee.*"

That evening, after she had sent an e-mail to Lois, Naomi pulled out the poster from the top of her rucksack. "Got to start somewhere," she said out loud as she turned the poster over and stuck some tape on each corner. Then she pressed the poster firmly to the wall next to her futon. It was a poster that showed, along with brightly coloured illustrations, the first seventy-six *kanji* characters that grade one children are taught in Japan.

It looks so juvenile, Naomi thought. *But I don't care. Learning Japanese is getting more and more interesting.*

九

The Youngest Schoolteacher

"Naomi, the children will be so excited to meet you. And they are all so sweet! It's hard to believe we were once so small," Keiko exclaimed excitedly as she watched Naomi prepare for her visit to Pippu Elementary School. "Of course," the woman added as an afterthought, "you're still small – young, that is."

Naomi smiled at Keiko's excitement, in spite of the giddy, nervous feeling in the pit of her stomach. Midori's father, who was the principal of the school, had invited Naomi to visit the grade three class. Word had got around town quickly; the children had been talking among themselves about the Canadian girl living in Pippu-cho and they were all very eager to meet her.

With a year of home-schooling ahead of her, Naomi felt it was nice to have something to do outside of the house, a place to go with a purpose. But she had never spoken in front of a large group before. There was the language barrier to consider, too; Naomi had to make sure her simple words were understood, through the use of all the maps and pictures she was bringing, as well as through her body language and gestures. The children would not understand every word she said, Naomi knew, but they would understand her overall meaning.

"I know what to do," she told herself forcefully, and rifled through the duffel bag in which she had carefully placed the things she wanted to show the children.

"Do you have everything?" Keiko asked.

"Let's see – map of Canada, picture book, flag, blackboard magnets, picture cards of me, Mom, Baba and Gigi, Lois and Imee, Billy, alphabet cards, number cards one to ten. Yes. That's everything," Naomi replied matter-of-factly.

"You are certainly prepared. Have a great time, Naomi. And remember, if you forget what to do, just get out the alphabet cards and sing the 'ABC Song.' They all know it, anyway – have fun!" Keiko gave the girl an approving glance and opened the front door for her. "Mr. Takenaka will be waiting for you in front of the school – it's only a fifteen-minute walk. Good luck, Naomi, I look forward to hearing all about your first school visit. Who knows, maybe you will grow up to be an English teacher like your mother."

As she walked to the school, Naomi went over her lesson plan for the tenth time. A fresh wave of nervousness overcame her as she approached the school and saw a man with thick glasses standing on the front steps. The man spotted her and bounded down the steps, his arm outstretched in a Western-style greeting.

"Hello, Naomi. I'm glad to meet you, finally. My daughter has told me a lot about you." The tall, bespectacled man spoke excellent English. He bowed forward slightly and reached to shake Naomi's hand at the same time, grinning broadly. "My name is Mr. Takenaka. Takenaka means 'in bamboo.' So, you can call me 'Mister In Bamboo.'" He and Naomi both laughed.

"Thank you, Takenaka-sensei," Naomi giggled as she replied, using the special term of honour, *sensei*, one uses when addressing teachers in Japan. "I'm glad to meet you, too. Midori has been really nice to show me around town and introduce me to her friends. And I'm looking forward to meeting some of your students here." Naomi began to relax, talking to this friendly, funny man.

Mr. Takenaka responded with eagerness, "Yes, the grade three students have been waiting all morning to meet you. Their teacher, Miss Ichimiya, told them you were coming. They have been practising saying 'Hello!' all morning." He laughed.

Naomi felt nervous as she took off her running shoes and placed them in the cupboard for visitors' street shoes. She selected a pair of slippers from among several lined up in the foyer. As she followed the principal down the corridor and up a flight of stairs, the oversized guest slippers threatened to flip right off her feet. Miss Ichimiya was waiting by the open door to the classroom.

"Ichimiya-sensei, this is *Now-mee*," Takenaka-sensei pronounced her name as his daughter Midori had told him to.

"Thank you for coming to my class, Naomi. The students are so excited," Naomi was surprised by the young-sounding voice of the grade three teacher.

"Have fun," Mr. Takenaka waved and was gone. Naomi timidly followed Miss Ichimiya into her classroom and found herself looking out over a room full of pink-cheeked, wide-eyed eight-year-old children sitting in columns of boy-girl pairs. Immediately, thirty-two small voices rose together in one big "OOOOOOOOOOh!" They wiggled around excitedly in their small chairs and began whispering to each other in Japanese:

"*Sugoi!* – Wow!" Naomi heard.

"She's tall," said one.

"Her nose is tall, too," said another.

Naomi suppressed a laugh. She was surprised and happy to discover she could understand a lot of what the children were saying. And the idea that, to Japanese eyes, Western people have "tall" noses was something her mother had mentioned to her years ago.

Miss Ichimiya explained to Naomi, "You are the first foreigner that most of these children have ever met. Overseas tourists don't often come to Pippu-cho. Most of them stay down south in Tokyo and Kyoto." She turned to the students and motioned for them to settle down in their seats.

"Students, we have a very special visitor today. This is Naomi Nazarevich," Miss Ichimiya stated to the class in Japanese, pronouncing her name the Japanese way: *Now-mee*. "Her mother is the new English teacher at Asahikawa Medical College. She comes from Canada. And I'm sure all of you have many questions you want to ask."

One small, mischievous-looking boy in the third row raised a hand.

"Yes, Shoji?" Miss Ichimiya asked.

He rattled off a stream of childish Japanese that Naomi could not understand. Miss Ichimiya listened to him, then turned to Naomi and said, "Shoji wants to know why you have a Japanese name."

"Oh," Naomi smiled and turned to look at Shoji. "My name is

Now-mee in Japanese. And in English, my name is 'Nay-oh-mee.'"
Miss Ichimiya translated for the class and nodded when she was
finished. Naomi found a piece of chalk on the ledge behind her and
wrote her name on the board. She then pointed to each letter as she
said it, and the children repeated after her: "N-A-O-M-I."

"*Nan sai desu ka?* – How old are you?" another student then asked.

Miss Ichimiya did not need to translate that simple question.
Naomi replied enthusiastically, "Twelve." She raised the ten fingers
on both her hands, and then followed this by raising two fingers on
her right hand, forming the well-known sign for peace. The students
laughed and copied this universal gesture in response.

"What is your favourite Japanese food?" asked one girl. She was
too shy to speak to Naomi, so she looked at Miss Ichimiya as she
spoke. Naomi waited for Miss Ichimiya to translate, even though she
understood this question as well.

"*Tempura, sukiyaki, sushi* ..." Naomi rattled off a list of her
favourites. There were so many she wasn't sure when to stop. Then
she paused and added dramatically, "*Shikashi* – But – *Konnyaku ga
kirai desu* – I don't like *konnyaku*." Naomi grimaced, shook her head
from side to side and waved her hands in front of her face animatedly.
The classroom rocked with laughter. The class's opinion of *konnyaku*
– a tasteless, jelly-like substance made from the root of the devil's
tongue plant, was mixed.

"*Konnyaku*. I don't like it, either." Naomi heard above the din and
saw a tall boy at the front of the class nod at her in agreement as he
spoke.

"Oh, but it's delicious," said his neighbour, a girl with two fat
braids, as she gave the boy a playful shove.

Miss Ichimiya spoke, "Students, let's play a game – 'Simon Says' –
with Naomi, okay?" After a few more words in Japanese, she turned
to Naomi and asked her to point to the parts of the body and say the
words. The children would repeat after her.

"Please stand up," Naomi said to the class as she raised her arms
in front of her, with her palms to the ceiling. The students rose together
on cue.

"Eye!" Naomi said loudly and clearly and pointed to her right
eye.

"Eye!" The children replied in unison and pointed to their eyes.

"Hair!" Naomi called out.

"Hair!" The children repeated after her.

"Nose!" she said.

"Nose!" the students chorused.

Naomi continued with "ear," "mouth," and "chin." She knew that six new words was enough for this first activity. She repeated all the words once again, more quickly, just to be sure they had understood, and then began the game. "Simon says touch your hair." Some of the students immediately touched their hair while the rest followed after only the slightest pause of uncertainty. It took quite some time for the number of players to dwindle, as those who incorrectly pointed to a body part when Naomi didn't say the magic words 'Simon Says' took their seats. Naomi marvelled at how clever they all were and how quickly they caught on. Eventually, only one student was left standing.

"Mika's the winner," Miss Ichimiya said and began to clap. All the students clapped as the young girl took her seat and grinned shyly at Naomi. At that moment, Naomi had an idea. She opened her duffel bag and pulled out a postcard of an RCMP officer of the famed Musical Ride, sitting proudly on his big black horse. She held it up for the class to see and then presented it to the little girl with a bow and a handshake. The other students clapped more loudly and the little girl beamed.

Then Miss Ichimiya asked Naomi, "Can you teach colours? The students know some of them."

"Sure," Naomi replied with confidence and faced the class. She pointed to her T-shirt. "Pink," she stated.

"Pink," the students chorused.

Naomi looked around the class and reached for a green notebook that lay on the teacher's desk. "Green," a few students shouted before Naomi had a chance to say the word.

"*Sugoi!* – Wow!" Naomi responded and praised the students. The students looked at each other happily. Then, Naomi pointed at her eye and leaned towards the mischievous-looking boy in the front row.

"Blue," the boy shouted, trying hard to pronounce the 'l' sound.

"Broo," the class chorused.

Then, from the back of the room, a student called out, "Yellow. Yellow hair."

Naomi laughed and reached for a lock of her hair. She scrunched up her face in a quizzical expression and asked, "Yellow? Is my hair yellow?" She exaggerated the intonation when she asked this, so the children knew that she was not making a statement, but asking them a question.

"Ah, *pinku?*" asked a little boy in Japanese.

"Blonde," Miss Ichimiya said, and asked the children to repeat this word carefully. The children had trouble pronouncing the 'l' in this word, as well.

Naomi added, "Yes – blonde – like your word, *kinpatsu*. But the *kin* in *kinpatsu* means 'gold.' My hair is a little different, don't you think?"

Naomi continued as Miss Ichimiya translated. "We have a special name for this colour of hair in English: strawberry blonde."

"Su-to-ro-be-ri," some of the students repeated. The word sounded familiar to them, for it is sometimes used in restaurant menus and advertising in Japan. Laughter began to erupt again in the classroom.

"*Ichigo?*" another student inquired, translating the word into Japanese.

"Yes, *ichigo*. Because my hair is a little bit red as well as blonde," Naomi answered and Miss Ichimiya translated.

"*Ichigo kinpatsu* – Su-to-ro-be-ri brond," another student said amid peals of laughter as he struggled with the 'l' sound.

Naomi blushed and felt her face grow pink like her T-shirt. She thought it would be a good time to talk about herself and show the pictures and the flag of Canada. She took the map from her bag and fastened it to the board with the magnets. Then she faced the class. "*Watashi wa Naomi* – I am Naomi. *Canada kara kimashita* – I come from Canada," Naomi continued, and circled the map with her finger. "*Portage la Prairie kara kimashita* – I come from Portage la Prairie," she pointed to the small point in the centre of the map. "It is a small town." She opened her big picture book on Canada to the page of the wheat field and the grain elevator and began walking between the columns of desks so all the children could see. "I live on the prairie – *daisogen*. We grow wheat – *mugi*," she pointed to the items as she spoke. "We grow potatoes and strawberries, too."

"Really? Just like in Pippu-cho!" Miss Ichimiya stated, with a surprised smile.

One small girl piped up and asked Miss Ichimiya with a big smile,

"Is Miss Naomi like Laura from the Little House on the Prairie?"

At once, everyone in the class burst into laughter, including Naomi and Miss Ichimiya. The little girl had addressed Naomi with the honoured term for teacher: *sensei!* And the little girl had imagined Naomi living a life like Laura Ingalls. Everyone knew about the adventures of the little girl named Laura and her life on the prairie.

The boy in the third row laughed as he replied, "Wrong! Miss Naomi is the strawberry blonde of Pippu Town." His classmates laughed even louder. Naomi and Miss Ichimiya laughed, too. Once she got over her giggles, Miss Ichimiya asked the students to settle down, and asked them a question to which they all responded with cries of joy. "The students would like you to stay for *kyushoku* — school lunch."

Had School Lunch, Got a New Nickname

"*I-ne!* – Good, isn't it! Su-to-ro-be-ri bronde-sensei is going to eat school lunch with us," Naomi understood some students say. Others clapped their hands with excitement. The school bell rang and all the students got up and began moving their desks into "islands" of six desks each. Some students began putting on white cotton overcoats, white cotton caps and even white surgical masks! It was all happening so fast, Naomi had to jump aside to avoid being run over by a group of children carrying big tin buckets of rice. Two more students had gone out into the hall and were returning with a plastic box containing thirty-four miniature glass bottles of milk.

Miss Ichimiya laughed at Naomi's speechless amazement. "You have never heard of school lunch in Japan? I hear it is very different from school lunch in Canada. We don't have a cafeteria here, and children do not need to bring their own food to school. All primary and junior-high-school students in Japan eat *kyushoku*."

"Neat!" Naomi exclaimed, as she watched the children bustling about, opening tin boxes, setting out stacks of bowls and spoons, while others began lining up with trays. "How does it work?"

Miss Ichimiya replied, "Well, every town in Japan has a "*Kyushoku* Centre" where the school lunches are made. At about noon, trucks deliver the food to all the primary and junior-high schools. The children collect the food from the delivery entrance and carry it back to their classrooms. All the buckets and boxes are labelled with a classroom number. It is all very organized." Miss Ichimiya turned and pointed to some posters on the bulletin board nearby. "This is the monthly duty roster for *kyushoku* for my class. Here it says which groups must serve the food, and who must clean up." Miss Ichimiya pointed to a calendar with tiny pictures. "And here, it shows what the menu is for each day."

Naomi traced with her finger to that day's date; it was easy enough to read, since the numbers were the same in Japanese. She could read the character for rice but couldn't understand the rest of it. "So today we're having rice and – "

"Yes, today's lunch is rice," Miss Ichimiya said with a smile, "and a special stew of beef, green beans, carrots, tofu and – "

"*Sensei! Sensei!*" a boy came up to Miss Ichimiya and began speaking with a worried expression on his face. Naomi didn't understand, but she thought she heard the word *konnyaku*. She smiled and had a hunch about what else was in today's stew.

Naomi looked down at the anxious boy and said in Japanese, "Maybe I will begin to like *konnyaku* from now on."

The boy, clearly relieved, scampered off and began preparing a tray of food for Naomi. Miss Ichimiya pulled a chair up to one island of desks and asked Naomi to sit down as the students brought over their lunch trays. At first, the six students at Naomi's "island" were too excited to eat, and they looked and smiled at Naomi and giggled to each other. Finally, one hungry boy opened his milk bottle, held it up, and said, "*Kampai.*"

The children and Naomi laughed and followed his lead. Naomi added the English translation "Cheers!" which the students repeated after her.

"*Tabemashoo* – Let's eat," another boy said as he dug into his bowl of stew.

"*Hai, tabemashoo* – Yes, let's eat," Naomi agreed as they all hungrily started in their school lunch. For dessert, they each had a large piece of mango, frozen in a plastic bag. She watched as the children opened the top of the bag and ate the piece of mango like she would a Popsicle.

After twenty minutes, the children began clearing up the lunch dishes. Bowls were scraped and the leftovers put back into the tin buckets. Miss Ichimiya explained to Naomi that the leftover food would not be wasted; it would be sent to the local pig farm. Desks were wiped clean and placed back into columns. Trays were stacked and milk bottles were returned to their container.

"Students, let's say thank you to Miss Naomi," Miss Ichimiya directed her class. In the middle of their cleanup activities, the children stopped and chorused, "Thank you!" One small voice said, "Bye-bye" and was soon followed by the whole class saying, "*Bye-bye Naomi-sensei! Bye-bye su-to-ro-be-ri bronde-sensei!*" The children waved and smiled brightly, excited by the chance to finally meet the girl from Canada.

"Bye-bye. See you again!" Naomi said and waved back happily. Miss Ichimiya and Naomi walked to the staff room, and Naomi felt relief and happiness. The class had gone great! The time had flown by! She hadn't even had time to talk about her family or sing the "ABC Song." *Oh, well. Maybe another time*, she thought as she continued down the corridor.

Miss Ichimiya's parting words interrupted Naomi's reverie, "Thank you, Naomi, for coming to visit my class. Please come again, and together we can teach them English. You can tell them more about Canada. They would like it very much." With a little wave, she turned to rejoin her students. Naomi skipped down the stairs to Takenaka-sensei's office and knocked on the door.

He opened the door. "Ah, Naomi-chan," he said, using the familiar term *chan* reserved for young girls, and motioned for Naomi to have a seat by his desk. "Did you have a nice class? Are my students clever? Are they polite? Do you like school lunch?"

Naomi sat down. "It was a great class. The children are all very *kawaii* – cute," she said, using another of the Japanese words from her growing repertoire. "And I loved the school lunch, even the *konnyaku!*"

"Good, good – it is very healthy for you." Takenaka-sensei replied. They continued to chat for a few minutes, then headed for the front entrance of the school, where Naomi removed her guest slippers and put on her street shoes. "Please come again to visit my students. You are welcome anytime," he said.

Naomi looked up at Takenaka-sensei and replied, "You have great students, Takenaka-sensei. I would love to come and visit them again."

"Well, we'll make the arrangements, then, if you're not too busy. Yes, my students are well-mannered – usually," he replied. After the slightest pause, he added, with twinkling eyes, "And I hear they have given you a new name: The Strawberry Blonde of Pippu-cho."

Wabi and Sabi – Calmness and Simplicity

"So this is where you've been hiding!" Sara said as she pulled aside the sliding glass doors leading to Keiko's second-floor balcony. It was already the middle of October and the autumn air had a real crispness in it.

"I come here a lot. This is my perch," Naomi replied. She inhaled deeply and looked over at the distant mountains to the south-east. "It's like you can almost smell the snow – somewhere out there."

Sara put her arm around her daughter and drew in a contented breath. She asked, almost tentatively, "Do you like it here, Naomi? I mean, are you beginning to like it here?"

Naomi looked over at her mother, noticing the hopeful look on her face. "I like it here, mom – I do. But I miss my friends. I miss everyone back home. It's like, it's just me and my home-schooling. I feel like I'm missing out. And there are no ballet classes for me to take here."

Sara nodded thoughtfully, "I know there's no ballet school in Pippu-cho. But that doesn't mean you have to stop practising, Naomi. And I know that making new friends is not the easiest thing in the world, but you've already got three – "

"But I miss Manitoba. Don't you?" Naomi interrupted.

"Of course I do, Naomi." Sara looked out over the little rice field nearby. The harvest was long past and the field was now bare and brown. It was a lonely sight. "But our home will always be there, Naomi. For now, why can't we think that, in our lives, our home will be a – bigger – place?"

Naomi snorted, "Sure, mom. A bigger place? We don't even live in our own place."

"That's not what I meant, Naomi," Sara cut in, hurt. She looked across at her daughter and her shoulders slumped. "What's wrong with you today?"

Naomi gave her mother a level gaze, then looked out at the fields again. "Lois hasn't e-mailed me in almost a week. I know they're all busy with school and making friends. Having all sorts of fun without me. Imee and Lois are forgetting about me."

Sara smiled sympathetically. "Naomi, I know your friends. You pick good friends. They may be busy at school, but they'll never forget about you." She put an arm around her daughter. "Keep yourself busy, and you won't miss them so much. And when you get back to Manitoba, you'll have that many more stories to tell them. They miss you. Baba and Gigi and Billy miss you. You know that."

Naomi wasn't convinced. So many times she had waited for a letter or an e-mail that never came. *Out of sight, out of mind, or so the saying goes. How does mom know, anyway?* She looked at her mother and was about to speak when Keiko entered the balcony, cheerful and serene as usual. "*Ohayo,*" she said brightly.

"Keiko-san, are you and Naomi going to have one of your little talks today?" Sara, sensing her daughter's unhappy mood, was eager to change the subject.

Keiko smiled across at Naomi, who had fixed her gaze back towards the mountains with a stubborn expression. The woman turned to Sara and smiled slightly. "Yes," she said, then added, "I think it is a good time to talk about the ideas of *wabi* and *sabi.*"

Sara's eyebrows shot up. "That's quite sophisticated, Keiko-san." Then, glancing back at Naomi, she added, "But I think it's a good idea." She leaned over to place a hand on Naomi's shoulder as she got up. "Well, I'm off to work now. Try to have a nice day, Naomi. And don't worry about your friends back home. Bye."

Keiko took a seat as Sara left. Naomi turned around to seat herself at the table, her eyes downcast. But her curiosity got the best of her and she asked, "What does *wabi* and *sabi* mean?"

"It does sound interesting, doesn't it?" Keiko's eyes twinkled. "To understand Japanese culture, and all its arts and traditions, one must understand the principle of *wabi-sabi*. To explain it simply, it has to do with the ideas of calmness and simplicity. These elements are reflected in everything from Japanese architecture to Japanese painting and design, how we prepare our food, and in traditional Japanese dance, poetry, theatre. Even our sports."

"What do you mean?" Naomi asked, puzzled.

Keiko looked out over the barren rice field and paused thoughtfully before turning back to Naomi. "*Wabi-sabi* can be translated as 'beauty in poverty.' But not the kind of poverty you are probably thinking."

Naomi was starting to feel discouraged, "I don't get it."

"Well, you have seen some traditional Japanese gardens. There are no bright colors – no flowers. Only rocks, and stones, a few trees. Maybe a pond. And yet it is a beautiful, peaceful place."

Naomi nodded, but she was not quite sure she understood.

Keiko smiled patiently. "Look at that old rice field, Naomi-chan. Tell me, how does it make you feel?"

Naomi looked out at the dried brown field again. "It looks – kind of sad. And lonely," she said simply.

"Do you like it?" asked Keiko.

"Yes, I do," Naomi replied. "It kind of reminds me of when I look out at the flat prairies in the middle of winter. It looks very lonely. But I feel a kind of – power, too. I think it's beautiful. In its own way."

Keiko nodded approvingly. "In Japan, it is said that we can find 'beauty in poverty' because, when we have nothing, we are forced to look inside ourselves. And when we do, we find the greatest beauty."

Naomi thought about what Keiko was saying. She looked at the rice field and visualized it in the spring, when it would be green once again. A small smile crept across her lips. "I think I understand."

"This idea is what makes Japanese traditions known all over the world for their simple beauty, grace and elegance. And harmony – an inner peace."

Naomi studied the woman who was sitting across from her. To her, Keiko was all these things. She was graceful and serene, but cheerful as well. *She always speaks to me like I am a real person*, Naomi thought to herself. Suddenly, Naomi felt ashamed for all the times she had shown her stubborn streak. "Keiko-san, I'm sorry that, sometimes, I am grumpy – like this morning. I would like to be graceful and elegant. More peaceful inside – like you say." She fiddled with the drawstring of her jacket. "It's just that – I miss home so much – I think about it a lot. I can't help it. I know my friends are forgetting about me. When I go home, my dog Billy probably won't even recognize me."

Keiko reached across the table and rested her hand on Naomi's arm. Naomi hesitated, then said, "When I practised my ballet back home, I would sometimes get this feeling – of being graceful and peaceful inside. I felt – light, somehow. Sometimes I would have to concentrate to keep the feeling." Her shoulders slumped. "But I don't have that feeling anymore. I worry about things a lot here."

Keiko was concerned. "You can get it back, Naomi, that special feeling. I am sure of that. It is just a matter of you deciding how you want to go about it."

"But there's no ballet school in Pippu-cho," Naomi replied glumly.

Keiko smiled, "Well, why don't you try something Japanese?"

"But all I know of is karate and judo. And that doesn't look very peaceful or elegant to me," Naomi replied.

Keiko laughed, "Well, Naomi. I can tell you that they are both very graceful when done correctly, although perhaps your mother would prefer that you try something else." Keiko and Naomi grinned at each other. "Actually, Naomi, have you heard of *kendo*?"

Naomi shook her head.

"*Kendo* means 'the way of the sword.' It is like Japanese-style fencing. The two players wear a special costume and they each hold a long bamboo stick – like a sword. But it's very safe." Naomi's eyes flickered with interest as Keiko continued, "The main principle in *kendo* is to keep your presence of mind – to stay calm and alert – rather than to injure the opponent. In Japan, *kendo* is often taught as basic training for all kinds of athletes. It is taught in school, and is quite popular with young people."

As Naomi pondered this, Keiko leaned forward and smiled broadly. "You know, Naomi-chan, I have an idea that would make any young girl happy – I think."

Naomi straightened up in her chair. "Oh? What's that?"

"Why don't you invite your three friends over for a party? I think those girls would love to be invited to a Halloween party. We don't really celebrate it here in Japan, although we all know about it."

"Would you let me have a party here?" Naomi's eyes lit up hopefully. "Could I invite Midori, Ai and Kiyoka – all three of them?"

"Of course, Naomi-chan!" Keiko replied warmly. "But there's just one thing. You have to invite me, too."

十二

t w e l v e

A Japanese Halloween

It was 6:30 p.m. on October 31 and the sky was already dark. A car stopped in front of Keiko's home. Midori, Kiyoka and Ai, all dressed in Halloween costumes, got out and started up the front walk, huddling together bashfully. The house looked dark.

"Waaaa!" Midori cried out in terror. The other girls glanced at her in alarm, then followed her frightened gaze to the front window.

"Kyaaa!" they gasped. There, in the window, a ghoulish face was staring at them. Suddenly, the face disappeared.

The girls sighed with relief. "*Sugoi!* – Bizarre!" Ai said, in slang Japanese.

The door was flung open and the ghoulish figure stood before them, immobile. The ghoul's mouth hung open in a big silent scream.

The elf grabbed the fairy to begin a hasty retreat back towards the street while the clown stood stock-still. The clown's eyes began to soften as the beginnings of a smile crept across her round face.

Naomi laughed as she pulled the mask off her head, and smiled back at the big clown standing in front of her on the doorstep. She looked over at the elf and the fairy who were now stopped, embarrassed, half-way across the front lawn. "Don't worry, it's me."

"Really, Naomi, that was a bit overdramatic, don't you think?" Sara said as she appeared, dressed as a witch, behind Naomi. She waved an arm, clad in a long black robe, and called out to Midori and Kiyoka, "Please come in – don't be afraid." Sara was a lovely witch, dressed in a flowing black gown. On her head she wore a wrinkled black cone-shaped hat, beneath which skeins of grey-wool hair tumbled out. Her face was tinted grey, and she had a big green wart on her nose.

As the girls filed through the door, the witch grinned broadly. The three girls did a double-take – was one of Sara's teeth missing? "*Kakko ii!* – Looks good!" Ai said and pointed to Sara's smile as they both burst out laughing.

Keiko, dressed as an old-fashioned Japanese peasant farmer, was waiting in the kitchen. "*Konbanwa* – Good evening. And happy Halloween," she said to the three colourful visitors.

"*Konbanwa*, Matsushita-san," Midori replied in a formal greeting, using Keiko's last name.

Naomi motioned for everyone to sit around the kitchen table, which was covered in sheets of newspaper. In the centre of the table stood a large orange pumpkin. Naomi and her mother had discovered that Japanese pumpkins were a lot smaller than Canadian ones. It had taken a lot of searching, but finally they had found a pumpkin to rival any grown in Manitoba. Next to each chair, there was one smaller pumpkin as well. The girls' eyes shone with expectation.

"You are a great clown," Sara said to Ai as Naomi brought over a tray of glasses and a pitcher of fruit punch. Naomi's mother looked over at Kiyoka. "You are a lovely fairy." Kiyoka beamed. Sara hesitated before addressing Midori, who looked as if she still hadn't gotten over her fright at the front door. Naomi smiled at Midori as she poured her a drink, and she heard her mother say, "You have a cute elf costume, Midori."

"What is 'elf'? I am not elf," Midori laughed, as did Ai and Kiyoka. Keiko was also laughing. Naomi and her mother looked at each other. Everyone obviously knew something they didn't! "I'm *Kerokerokeroppi*," she said to more laughter all around the table.

Keiko explained, "'*Kerokerokeroppi*' is a frog – a very popular character, like 'Hello Kitty,' or 'Mickey Mouse.'" Naomi and her mother began to understand. They knew that Japanese people of all ages loved these cute characters. There were many of them, and they could be found on everything from pencil-cases and school notebooks to wallpaper and even credit cards!

"Let's make Jack-o'-lanterns and pumpkin pie," Naomi said.

"Pumpkin pie?" Ai asked. Midori and Kiyoka giggled.

Once again, Keiko explained. "Pumpkin pie is not common in Japan. Most Japanese people only eat it as a savoury dish, cooked with soy sauce. "

"No pumpkin pie?" Naomi asked, surprised. "In Canada, we love pumpkin pie." She reached for a black felt marker. "First, we'll draw a face on the pumpkins." She gestured to show the meaning of her words in case her friends didn't understand.

The girls had fun trying out different faces by drawing them on the newspaper that was spread out over the table. Their own faces were a study in concentration as they began to draw the eyes, noses and mouths on their Jack-o'-lanterns. When they were done drawing the faces, Sara carefully cut the tops off the pumpkins, giving each one a distinctive hairline in the process. Ai had given her Jack-o'-lantern big round eyes and high eyebrows to go with a wide mouth, giving it a surprised appearance. Midori's and Naomi's Jack-o'-lanterns looked similar, with dangerous-looking eyes and intimidating frowns. Kiyoka's pumpkin had the familiar-looking triangles for eyes. Its mouth was a large, zig-zag grin.

The girls laughed and joked as they scooped out the insides of the pumpkins with big spoons and placed the slimy orange contents in a large bowl. When they were finished, Naomi brought a baking tray lined with aluminum foil to the table and asked them to help separate the large slippery pumpkin seeds from the slimy, stringy pulp. After all the pumpkin seeds had been placed on the tray, Naomi sprinkled salt over them and placed them in the oven. Meanwhile, Keiko and Sara had cut out the eyes, nose and mouth of everyone's Jack-o'-lantern, as well as the large centrepiece pumpkin.

"Now, let's make some pumpkin pie," Naomi said excitedly. She loved fruit pies, but pumpkin had to be her favourite pie of all. She hefted the big glass bowl of pumpkin pulp and carried it into the kitchen, her three friends close behind. Several glass bowls, a mix-master, and all the ingredients for the pie had been laid out on the kitchen counter. Four empty pie crusts waited on a shelf nearby. Naomi scooped the pulp into the largest bowl. Each girl ceremoniously dropped in the other ingredients: eggs, milk, sugar, and a little cooking oil. Together, the four girls huddled over the bowl and watched in silence as the lumpy mixture spun in the mix-master, soon turning into a smooth batter. Naomi hefted the bowl into her arms and poured the mixture into the empty pie shells.

The kitchen was filled with the sweet aroma of the pie filling. As Keiko opened the oven door to remove the tray of roasted pumpkin seeds, a warm salty scent mingled with the sweetness of the uncooked pies. Keiko shook the seeds on the baking tray and then poured them into a wooden bowl lined with decorative orange and black paper.

Naomi asked Midori to carry the bowl of freshly roasted pumpkin seeds, and the four girls returned to the kitchen table to collect their drinks. Naomi led her friends into the living room. The girls rounded the corner and gasped in awe. The lights were off – all they could see were the one large and four small Jack-o'-lantern faces glowing at them, with expressions ranging from surprise, to fear, to anger – and plain old silliness!

"*Tanoshii!* – Fun!" Midori cried out, and giggled her special little giggle.

Naomi's mother switched on the light and said, "In Canada, we put our Jack-o'-lanterns in the front window, for everyone to see."

The girls sat on the floor in the living room around the large square coffee table, now sporting a quilted skirt around the edge. The girls snuggled their legs under the table's skirt and soon felt the heat radiating from a small heater attached to the underside of the table. "In Canada, we don't have *kotatsu*," Naomi said, referring to this interesting piece of Japanese furniture. "It's a great idea. Manitoba is very cold in the winter. We sure could use one of these. But I don't know if Baba and Gigi could sit on the floor." Naomi laughed as she pictured her tall grandfather trying to cross his big legs under the low *kotatsu*.

"Who is Baba and Gigi?" asked Midori, confused.

"Baba and Gigi are my grandmother and grandfather," Naomi replied.

"Ah – *Obaasan* and *Ojiisan*," Midori translated for Kiyoka and Ai. All four girls immediately noticed the similar sounds of these words, which shared the same meaning in English and Japanese. They looked at each with surprised expressions.

"Baba is *Obaasan* – " Kiyoka began.

"Gigi is *Ojiisan*," Midori finished.

"That's so neat! Almost the same words in English and Japanese," Naomi commented. They were amazed at this odd discovery, sipping their drinks and munching the delicious salted pumpkin seeds, still warm from the oven. Keiko came in with a small pile of multicoloured papers. She spoke in Japanese to Naomi's friends, who nodded and smiled.

"We teach you *origami*," Ai said, and passed a paper to each girl. She waved her paper in the air. "*Origami* number one. Let's make – *tsuru*," she said.

Naomi watched as the girls expertly folded their papers this way and that. Within a minute, each girl was holding a small, perfectly shaped paper crane. Naomi was impressed. "Okay. More slowly, please," she said, as the three girls laughed and reached for more paper. Naomi's first crane was a raggedy-looking bird, but by the third attempt, neither Sara nor Keiko could tell which one was hers. Kiyoka showed Naomi how to make a small box, and Midori taught her how to make a frog that, when pressed with a finger, would hop away.

Naomi had an idea. She got up from the table and went into the kitchen, where her mother and Keiko were chatting happily over cups of tea. "Keiko-san, may I have an old newspaper, please?"

Keiko handed Naomi the morning paper and she quickly rejoined her friends. She passed each of them a double-spread page. "I know how to do a hat," she said triumphantly, and began carefully folding off an edge to make a square. The girls watched and followed her lead. Within minutes, each girl had made a large paper hat. Ai plunked hers down on top of her head, and posed coyly.

"Looks good," declared Kiyoka, and the other girls nodded in agreement.

They were so absorbed in their paper-folding that they didn't notice the delicious smell of the baking pie until it was brought into the room by Keiko and Sara. Ai and Midori squeezed together to make room at the little table for them both.

"Let's eat," Naomi said as the girls dug into their pieces of pie. There were a few moments of silence before the verdict was known.

Kiyoka's eyes widened. "*Oooiiishiii!* – Delicious!" she declared.

"*Oishii, ne?* – Good, isn't it?" Naomi said, and giggled. She thought the word *oishii* sounded – well – delicious. She was beginning to use it more and more.

"Delicious," Ai said as she focused on her pie for another bite.

At ten o'clock, Sara suggested that it was time to drive the girls home. Naomi and her mother brought out four boxes. "In Canada, we give candies on Halloween. But today, we will give you some pumpkin pie," Naomi said.

Each girl happily accepted a small box, with a little bow. Then Naomi and her mother blew out the candles on the pumpkins, and carried them out to the car. Ai jumped up in excitement when she realized that she would get to keep the Jack-o'-lantern she had made, and then quickly stopped jumping when Kiyoka reminded her that she was still holding a box of pie in her hands. The girls went home pleased and excited, secretly hoping that it wouldn't be too long before they could celebrate Halloween again.

Snuggled in her futon that night, Naomi thought about her Halloween party. *It wasn't a big party, like the kind I used to have, and be invited to, with my friends back in Portage la Prairie... But that's okay. I had a good time – and so did my friends.* She drew the fluffy covers up closer around her shoulders. The wind was howling, but she felt warm and contented. She looked over at her bedroom windowsill, to her small Jack-o'-lantern. In the window pane, she noticed the reflection of its face, lit up by the candle inside, and wondered how many passers-by would see it. The wind howled louder. Winter was well on its way, but around Pippu-cho, four small Jack-o'-lanterns lit a patch of warmth into the dark night.

Email to: schulz@goforit.mb.net
From: nazarevich@arc-net.co.jp
Subject: Happy Halloween!

Dear Lois (and Imee),
    How are you doing? I'm doing fine. I had a Halloween party today. It wasn't very big, I only had three friends to invite, but we had fun. How's school going? I still can't believe I'm not there with you. Tell me all about it!
    See you soon. Don't forget I'm coming home for Christmas! I can't wait to see you all. Maybe we can go on another hay ride! Bye, Lois. Please share this e-mail with Imee.

    Love, Naomi

thirteen

The Eye of the Daruma Doll

"Takenaka-sensei, what is a *cho*?" Naomi asked.

Perplexed by her question, Mr. Takenaka put down his chopsticks. He looked first to Naomi and then across the table to his daughter, Midori. Equally puzzled, Midori shrugged her shoulders.

"*Cho*? You are talking about a Japanese word, Naomi?" he asked. She nodded. "Well, Naomi, you know that the Japanese language has many words that sound the same. In English, you call them 'homonyms.' In Japanese, there are so many of these homonyms that sometimes we need to see the Chinese character – the *kanji* – before we can understand what someone is talking about." Mr. Takenaka paused, then chuckled, "There are many *cho*'s in the Japanese language. You'll have to give me a clue."

"You know, *cho* – Pippu-*cho*," Naomi replied matter-of-factly.

Midori answered, "Oh – Pippu-*cho*. Easy! *Cho* means 'town.'"

Naomi nodded, she was expecting to hear that. "Yes, I thought that *cho* meant town. But when I went to Furano, the sign said: Welcome to Furano-*machi*. Furano is a town, too. So then I thought: Why is Pippu a *cho*, but Furano a *machi*?"

"*Machi* means 'town,' too," Midori replied happily.

Naomi thought about this and looked at everyone seated around the table. Couldn't they see the problem? "Well, what's the difference between a *cho* and a *machi*, then?"

"Ah, Naomi-chan, that is a very good question," Mr. Takenaka said. "You know, sometimes there is no exact translation between one language and another."

Naomi nodded. She was well aware of that! She could think of many examples of this: like the popular word *gaman*, which was translated in her dictionary as "endure." She knew that this word was a sort of all-purpose word for "Keep going," "Chin up!" or some sort of encouragement like that. And then there was *genki*, a word Naomi, and everyone else in Japan, loved to use. People would often ask her in greeting: *Genki desuka?*, meaning "Are you active and healthy and happy?" Naomi would always smile and say: *Genki desu!*

"I think the word *genki* is a good example of that," Naomi said. "We don't really have a word like that in English."

"That's a very good example, Naomi-chan," Mr. Takenaka replied. "Can you think of any others?" he asked and looked around the table.

After a brief pause, Midori spoke up, "*Ganbatte*. We say this a lot. Naomi says it's not easy to translate into English."

"Yes. Mom told me that *ganbatte* means "You can do it!" I heard that a lot at your school sports day, Midori," Naomi said, enjoying the conversation. "When I was in grade four at school, our class did a project on the Canadian Inuit. My teacher told us that that the Inuit have many different ways to say the word 'snow.'" She tried to remember what she had learned, "One word might mean 'the first snow of the year.' Another might mean 'sticky snow.' Like that."

Mr. Takenaka was impressed. "That's very interesting. It tells us that snow is very important in their lives. You see, by studying a language, you can learn more about a country – or a people."

Naomi looked down at her plate. "I don't think my Japanese will ever be good enough for that," she said wistfully. "I've been here for over three months now, and I can't speak very well. I can say greetings and talk about the weather and small things; where I am going and what I am doing – "

Mrs. Takenaka smiled sympathetically over at Naomi, "Naomi, three months is not a long time. My husband and I have spent almost all our lives learning English. We are still learning. When we talk to you, for example, we learn something new." She looked across at her husband.

"I want to learn English more," Midori said.

"I want to learn Japanese more, too," Naomi said. Both girls laughed.

"Teach each other. There are many ways to learn a language," Mrs. Takenaka said. "When we lived in Michigan, I would listen to the radio."

"And every night we would listen to the news on television. After a while, we could understand most of it," Takenaka-sensei added. "When we returned to Japan, my wife and I made a promise to keep using our English as much as we could. Not many people speak English in Pippu-cho, but there is an English Club in Asahikawa."

Mrs. Takenaka looked at Midori, "We want you to improve your English. When Naomi-chan is here, we will all do our best to speak in English."

"No problem," Midori replied and everyone chuckled. Naomi knew that this was probably the most well-known English phrase in all of Japan – after "Do you like sushi?"

Takenaka-sensei said, "One thing I liked to do to practise my English, when I lived in Michigan, was to write poetry. I still do it."

"You write poetry – in English?" Naomi asked, surprised.

"I write a special kind of poetry: *haiku*. Do you know about it?"

"Oh yes. We wrote English *haiku* poems at school in Manitoba – I remember! It has a special pattern," Naomi said, scrunching up her face as she tried to recall, "Something like: seven-five-seven. Am I right?"

Takenaka-sensei laughed, "You're almost correct. The pattern is five syllables, then seven, then five again. *Haiku* poems are short."

"In English, you say 'Less is more.' That is the feeling we have about *haiku*," Mrs. Takenaka added.

"*Haiku* is very important in traditional Japanese culture," Mr. Takenaka explained. "Do you know who wrote the very first *haiku* poem, Naomi?" As she shook her head, he looked over to Midori and raised his eyebrows.

Midori laughed and answered the question that most Japanese children know well: "Basho."

"And can you say one of his poems?" her father asked.

Midori sat straight in her chair and recited some melodious Japanese:

> kareeda ni
> karasu no tomarikeri
> aki no kure

To Naomi, it sounded beautiful. "What does it mean?" she asked.

"It's about autumn," Midori answered. "Most *haiku* are about seasons."

Takenaka-sensei put down his napkin, looking proudly at Midori. Then he chuckled. "That's very good, Midori. That is one of Basho's best *haiku* poems. But that one has eighteen syllables." He looked over at Naomi, "I think Basho was using what you call 'artistic licence.'" Then he sat forward in his chair, leaning closer to Naomi and Midori. "I have an idea. Why don't you try to translate that poem together? Look up the words and write your own English version. I'll give you one hour. If you can do it in less than one hour, I will ..." he thought about this and looked at his wife. "Well, I don't know. But I will have to do something special, if you can do it," he finished, laughing.

Naomi and Midori looked at each other. It was an interesting challenge for them both. "Okay, Naomi. Let's go to my bedroom," Midori said.

The two girls excused themselves. "*Gochisosama deshita,*" Naomi said as she pushed her chair back from the table. She loved to say those words. Keiko had taught her to say them at the end of a meal. Translated directly into English, it meant: "It was an honourable good meal," and was a way of complimenting the hostess.

Mrs. Takenaka smiled and said, "My, you are learning to be very Japanese, Naomi-chan."

"*Domo arigato,*" Naomi said, bowing mischievously before following her friend to the bedroom.

Midori grabbed her Hello Kitty alarm clock. "Pens, paper, dictionary," she said as she pulled open her desk drawer. The girls tumbled onto Midori's Western-style bed, reminding Naomi that it had been a long time since she had slept in one. Midori repeated the poem and wrote the Japanese words in *hiragana* on a piece of paper. Naomi, watching over her friend's shoulder, was reminded once again how different Japanese and English writing were. It was fascinating to watch Midori writing her words in vertical columns, starting from the top right of the page, working her way down, then moving to the left to start another column at the top.

Midori's voice cut in, "*Kareeda* – it's a branch of an old, dead tree." There was the word *karasu*. "Is it a crow?" Naomi asked as she thumbed through her own well-used pocket dictionary. "Yes, crow," she answered herself and, grabbing another piece of paper, she began to write.

"*Tomarikeri* means 'to sit' – like a bird sits on a branch," Midori said.

"Okay, Midori. And *aki* means autumn – *kure* means – here it is ..." she showed the dictionary entry to Midori, who carefully read it: dusk, night.

Naomi wrote the last of the words down as Midori hovered over her:

> *a crow is sitting*
> *on a dead and withered branch*
> *an autumn night*

They reread their translation of Basho's poem, pleased with themselves. Then, with a look of consternation, Naomi pointed to the last line and said, "We need one more syllable." Within minutes, they had rewritten the poem:

> a *crow is sitting*
> *on a dead and withered branch*
> *the autumn twilight*

"*Yatta!* – We did it! Only twenty-five minutes!" Midori exclaimed. They practised reciting the poem together one last time before heading to the living room.

"So, have you discovered the meaning of the poem?" Mr. Takenaka asked with interest as he put down his newspaper.

"Yes. We hope you like it," Naomi replied. Giving each other the signal to start, the two girls recited the poem in unison.

Takenaka-sensei looked first at his wife and then at the girls. He was clearly impressed. "That's very good. Really." He studied them for a few moments and then flipped through the newspaper. "I'm looking – ah, here it is." He laid the newspaper out on the coffee table. "Midori, Naomi – come over here. You may be interested in this." Naomi looked at the newspaper, one of Japan's English dailies. She read the headline:

"Oh!" Naomi exclaimed with delight, "It's an English *haiku* contest! I love contests." She kneeled on the floor to get a closer look at the winning poem. "You're right. I *am* interested." She read the winning poem aloud:

my clock says six
I can stay in bed longer
my favourite time

Naomi looked at the page in puzzled amusement. Midori smirked. Mr. Takenaka said, "You can do better, I think. Both of you."

"Yes. I think I'll give it a try. What about you, Midori?"

Midori nodded. "Me, too," she said.

Mr. Takenaka went to a cupboard and took out a box, setting it on the coffee table. He motioned for Midori to open it. Smiling, she lifted something out and placed it in front of Naomi. "This is a Daruma doll," Midori explained.

Naomi looked at the Daruma doll. She had not seen anything like it. It was oval, about eight inches high. She guessed it was made of paper maché. The doll was painted in a bright pattern of red, white and black.

"Why doesn't the doll have any eyes?" asked Naomi.

"Ah – this is part of the Daruma doll tradition, Naomi," Takenaka-sensei answered in his scholarly way. "You see, the Daruma doll will give you luck. If you want to accomplish something, you get a Daruma doll and paint in one of the eyes – "

Naomi guessed what he was going to say next.

"And when you achieve your goal, you paint in the other eye – and celebrate," he finished happily. He rose again from his chair and returned moments later with another small, elegantly decorated box. He brought out a heavy black stone, a small glass bottle, and a paint brush. Naomi watched as he appeared to lift off the top half of the stone, revealing a shallow recess. He poured some black ink onto the stone, and, dipping the paintbrush lightly in the ink, he presented it to Naomi.

Carefully, Naomi took the brush and painted in a big black circle where the left eye was supposed to be. "Is this okay?" she asked.

Takenaka-sensei nodded. "Now," he said, grinning broadly. "When both of you get a poem in the newspaper, we can paint in the other eye."

On her futon that night, Naomi opened her diary to a fresh page and held her pen above it, thinking of an idea for a *haiku* poem. For several minutes, she sat motionless, and then, it was as if her hand was writing by itself:

> *alone in the dark*
> *a Canadian satellite*
> *spins over Japan*

She stopped and stared at what she had just written. *What's that supposed to mean?* she thought. But in her heart, Naomi knew.

十 四

f o u r t e e n

First-day Jitters

"You have to think I look a little dorky in this outfit, huh?" Naomi asked, studying her reflection in the mirror. Her mother tilted her head to one side, studying Naomi's reflection. A slow smile spread across her face. "Well, put it this way. You may get looks if you were back in Portage la Prairie but, as they say, "When in Rome – "

"Do as the Romans do," Naomi finished with a grimace, and took a deep breath. "I'm nervous. I can't believe I'm actually going to be a student in a Japanese junior-high school. If Imee and Lois – and Baba and Gigi – could see me now," she said as she pirouetted in front of her mother and Keiko. Today was Naomi's first day as a student at Pippu Junior-High School.

"I think it's neat," Sara stated. "Naomi, you'll have to thank Takenaka-sensei for putting in a good word with the school board, although he said it didn't take a lot of convincing. The principal liked the idea. Apparently, he thought having a Canadian girl at his school would help the students become more – international."

"*Kokusai ka*," Naomi enunciated carefully, and then said its English translation, "Internationalization." It was a well-known word in Japan. "I'm happy to do my bit for internationalization."

Keiko laughed, and said, "You'll have a good time, Naomi-chan. You'll meet a lot of new friends your age."

"I hope so. I hope that things won't be too difficult," she replied.

89

A thought furrowed her brow, "I hope that they won't pick on me because I'm different from them, and can't speak Japanese very well."

Keiko came over and squeezed the girl's shoulders encouragingly, but her eyes showed concern. "You may find that some of the students may not behave – in their best way. At least at first," Keiko said. "But try to understand. Children – adults too – often don't know how to react when they are faced with something new. People need time to adjust. Japan is not like Canada, you know, where people have come to live from all over the world, like Ukraine."

Naomi blushed, thinking back to her own negative behaviour when she first came to Japan, and her first reaction to being called an "outsider."

"I remember when I was in junior-high school," Sara said. "There was a clique of girls who decided they didn't like me. I never found out why. Anyway, when I realized that they were trying to not be friendly to me – on purpose – it bothered me a lot." She glanced over at the photograph of her parents on the desk. "But then my mom said something that I've never forgotten. She said "Nobody can be everyone's best friend.'" Sara adjusted the barrette in Naomi's hair. "So, Naomi, just enjoy the friends you have, and the ones you're going to make. And don't worry about the rest." She gave her daughter a hug, and they smiled at each other's reflection in the mirror. "You just keep on being you, Naomi, and you'll be fine."

Nobody can be everyone's best friend. It wasn't a fairy-tale ending, but Naomi knew that what Baba had said was honest. She smiled, slightly. *I can live with that,* she thought. *Besides, I like the friends I have, and maybe I'll make some more.* She turned to give her mother a big hug in return.

"Just enjoy yourself, Naomi-chan, and try to do your best. That's all anyone can do," Keiko said, then added approvingly, "You look lovely."

Naomi surveyed herself in the full-length mirror. *This sure isn't what kids my age wear to school in Manitoba,* she thought, but she had to admit, the Japanese winter uniform was formal, yet nice: a navy wool sailor jacket over a knee-length pleated navy skirt. Fitted under the large square collar of the jacket was a white scarf that tied in the front. On her feet, Naomi wore knee-length white socks, pulled tightly.

How different she looked from the Portage la Prairie girl of just a few months ago, in jeans and a T-shirt. Now, she was heading to a

Japanese school, three times a week. She put her hand on her stomach to steady her nerves. She had even worse jitters than she'd had on her first day of school in Portage la Prairie last year. *Will they like me? I hope I don't make a fool of myself,* she thought.

"Naomi, everything is going to be fine," her mother said, and rested a hand on her shoulder. "Like Keiko-san says, just enjoy yourself. It's an experience that few girls from Manitoba ever get."

Naomi gulped. "Easier said than done," she replied, then reminded herself, *This was my idea, so now I've gotta just do it.*

With a deep breath and a wave to her mother and Keiko, Naomi shouldered her rucksack and headed out the door. The air was chilly, and the bright sun had only its weak November warmth to offer. Naomi shivered to warm herself. "Nobody can be everyone's best friend. Just keep being me." she said under her breath, and then, "Just another first day of school in the life of Naomi Nazarevich." She groaned, and then stopped to pull up a sock that was starting to slip down her leg. "Pull up your socks."

Naomi could tell she was getting closer to the school as she began to see more and more students in the familiar navy and black uniforms heading in the same direction. All of them were clustered in small groups and pairs. She could feel their eyes on her as she walked along. The feelings of nervousness did not go away. Instead, they seemed to be getting worse with each step nearer to Pippu Junior-High School. *Maybe this idea about me going to school part-time wasn't such a good idea after all,* she thought. A group of boys ran past her on the sidewalk, shoving each other jokingly. One of the boys looked over his shoulder at Naomi and laughed.

Naomi hung her head. Her cheeks burned. *They're laughing at me, just like those little boys in the park,* she thought. All of a sudden, she felt glad that no one from Canada could see her now. She looked up and could see the gates of the school at the end of the block. The babble of students' voices grew louder as she approached the school gate. Naomi felt that knot of fear in her stomach again. It was getting bigger. She stopped in her tracks. *I could turn around and head straight back home. Mom would understand if I changed my mind,* she told herself, and she began to turn on her heel. Then, among the sea of dark school uniforms, Naomi spotted movement inside the school grounds. She focused, and saw Ai, waving her arms, trying to get her attention. Then Kiyoka and Midori began motioning for Naomi to come through the gate. Kiyoka was moving forward. Naomi stood frozen. *If I leave right now, I can pretend I never saw them*, she thought. The girls continued waving. She could see several students standing beside her three friends, looking in her direction. *I've been spotted — can't turn back now!*

十五

f i f t e e n

Kendo –
The Way of the Sword

Naomi took a deep breath and walked through the gates of the school with the rest of the stragglers, who were now running to get to school before the eight o'clock bell. Midori, Ai and Kiyoka grabbed her arms excitedly.

"We are waiting for you," said Ai, grinning broadly.

Kiyoka nodded and said, "You look nice, Naomi-chan."

The bell rang out the familiar "Big Ben" sound. Ai grabbed Naomi's elbow and practically pulled her through the door. Other girls crowded around Ai, Kiyoka and Midori, staring at Naomi and whispering things in Japanese. The sounds of laughter and a babble of Japanese echoed in her ears. She concentrated on the stairs and could hear Ai answering the other students' questions authoritatively in Japanese: "Her name is Naomi – it really is. She comes from Canada. She's a part-time student. Monday, Wednesday, Friday." Naomi was relieved to find that she understood a lot of what her friend was saying. Then, inexplicably, she felt tears start to sting her eyes.

Midori whispered sympathetically, "Don't worry, Naomi. We are in the same class."

"*Dekiru yo* – You can do it, Naomi-chan," Kiyoka said quietly as they walked down the hall. "Our homeroom teacher is Miss Toyoda.

93

She is an English teacher."

Naomi looked up at her friends. The look on their faces was a mix of encouragement and excitement. *I can do this*, she told herself. She said it out loud, "Yes, I can do this." Her eyes stopped stinging and the knot of anxiety in her stomach beat a hasty retreat.

Most of her classmates were already seated at their desks when Naomi arrived at the classroom. All the chatter stopped when she entered the room. Naomi could feel thirty pairs of eyes focused on her as Midori led her to the empty desk behind her own. She sat down and began to put her books and gym clothes into her desk. A murmur of Japanese started up again: "Where does she come from? What's her name?" There were a few snickers. Naomi's head began to buzz when she heard the word *gaijin* again. She looked up and saw two girls staring at her from two rows over. They looked at her with cool, blank expressions, then giggled and whispered to each other behind their hands. Midori followed Naomi's gaze and a worried look came over her. Then the homeroom teacher, Miss Toyoda, entered the class and the murmuring and giggling stopped. Miss Toyoda looked rather severe. Naomi's heart sank.

Miss Toyoda looked straight at Naomi as she stood at the front of the classroom. Then she looked around the room and spoke sternly to her class in Japanese. *What's she saying?* Naomi wondered. It sounded bad.

"Good morning, Naomi. Welcome to Pippu Junior-High School," Naomi heard the classroom chorus. Startled, she looked up and saw that everyone was looking at her. Their eyes were solemn; instructed by their teacher, they were making an effort to welcome Naomi in English. They had just been told that they would have to be more diligent in English, now, and that Naomi was to be treated as a regular fellow student. Naomi looked at the faces around her. Some were excited. She glanced quickly at the two mean-looking girls, and saw that they were still staring at her with that look of contempt. She gulped. She spotted Ai two rows away and Kiyoka clear across the room, smiling encouragingly.

"Naomi, would you like to say anything to my students?" Miss Toyoda asked. Naomi was sure she hadn't seen a smile cross the teacher's face yet. She stood up shakily and looked at Midori seated in front of her.

"You can do it," Midori whispered.

94

"*Konnichiwa, minnasan* – Hello, everyone ..." Naomi began.

"Oooooooh," the boys, and some of the girls, crooned in unison. Laughter filled the room.

"*Watashi wa Naomi Nazarevich. Canada kara kimashita* – I am Naomi Nazarevich. I come from Canada," Naomi continued, and then began to say a few lines in Japanese that she and Keiko had worked on the night before. "I will be coming here Monday, Wednesday and Friday mornings." Naomi stopped. Her mind was blank. She had forgotten the rest of the words she had memorized. "I hope you'll help me out," she stammered out quickly in Japanese, and sat down.

"Ooooooooh."

"Enough!" Miss Toyoda barked at the rowdier students, then added, "Thank you, Naomi. We hope you will help us all improve our English." Miss Toyoda spoke with a faint British accent, and she cast a reproachful glance around the classroom. The bell signalling the first class chimed. Miss Toyoda continued in Japanese, "Now, let's start with *kokugo* – Japanese language class. Take out your books." Immediately the students began pulling notebooks out of their desks. But from her seat at the back, Naomi could see some of the students were still giving her cool, appraising glances, and then grinning secret grins at each other across the rows of desks. Naomi pulled out her own books for studying Japanese writing. She was glad for the opportunity to immerse herself in the study of *kanji*. She felt trapped, desperate to remove herself from this class full of strange people, if only in her mind. *At least I can study on my own if I can't follow what's in the class*, Naomi reassured herself as Miss Toyoda began writing a series of *kanji* across the board for the class to copy.

When the bell rang, Naomi looked up at the clock with a feeling of immense relief. *That forty-five minute class went by pretty quickly*, she thought. Midori, Ai, Kiyoka, and a few other students came over to Naomi's desk to look at the characters she had written in her notebook.

"Very good," Ai said.

A tall boy pushed in between Ai and another girl to look at Naomi's notebook, "Vwery gooood! Vwery goooood!" he said, mimicking Ai. The other girls burst into giggles and the boys hooted.

Naomi snapped her notebook shut. *I'm not a monkey in a zoo,* she thought to herself as she looked up at the nosy boys and girls crowding around her desk. The boy caught Naomi's eye in mid-guffaw. The grin stopped and his eyes widened. Naomi thought she could see a red flush rise from the stiff collar of his school uniform, right up to his short-cropped hair. He took a deep breath and put out his hand. "I am Kenji."

"Oooooooh," some students began again.

Kenji waved them off, then turned to face Naomi once again. He leaned forward and took another deep breath. "Aaah – do you like sushi?" he asked, finally.

"Oooooooh."

Kenji turned to face the class and spoke in forceful Japanese. At once, the giggling girls and the noisy boys stopped joking around. Naomi was impressed. "I like *tekka-maki*," she replied, referring to the popular rolls made of raw tuna inside rice and wrapped in sheets of seaweed called *nori*.

Kenji nodded. He pointed to his chest and said, "I like *inari-zushi*." Naomi smiled. She knew what that was; rice wrapped in sheets of sweetened fried tofu. Keiko referred to it as "football sushi" because of its shape.

Ai coolly brushed Kenji aside and said to Naomi, "We have P.E. now. Let's go." Naomi got up to follow the rest of the girls in the class. Just as she reached the doorway, she heard Kenji say, "I like *tekka-maki*, too." Naomi turned around and looked at Kenji's happy face. *So this is what mom calls "cross-cultural communication,"* she thought, and grinned.

Ai, Kiyoka and Midori huddled together with Naomi as they made their way to the gym. "Did you like *kokugo* class?" Midori asked.

"*Kokugo* is interesting," said Naomi. "I like studying *kanji*. I know about two hundred, now."

"*Jozu*, Naomi-chan. You are great!" exclaimed Midori.

The girls were shivering in their gym clothes as they waited for the teacher to arrive. Naomi couldn't believe how cold it was in the huge open space. Across the room, the boys were dribbling basketballs. She watched as Kenji took a run up to the basket. He missed. The other boys teased him, and he tried another, successful, attempt. Naomi smiled.

"Today, we start to learn kendo," said Midori.

Naomi's ears pricked up. The girls' gym teacher emerged from the storage room, her arms loaded down with what looked like long sticks of bamboo – *shinai*. The kendo outfits had four main parts: a helmet, called *men*; protective wrist and hand coverings, *kote*; a breastplate, *do*; and waist protection, *tare*. Mrs. Wada then went on to explain basic stances and movements. With Midori's help, Naomi was able to understand that the idea is to score two points within a three-minute time limit. A point is scored by attacking certain areas of the head, wrist, and torso. Naomi watched, fascinated, as Mrs. Wada took one of the bamboo "swords" and demonstrated its proper usage.

The gym teacher asked the girls to pick a partner. Ai grabbed Naomi's arm. Standing across from each other, each pair watched and followed the teacher's movements. They practised the basic steps repeatedly for ten minutes, then moved into actual short matches. Naomi laughed at Ai's clowning behind the gym teacher's back. With ten minutes left in the class, Mrs. Wada blew her whistle and asked for some volunteers for a more formal match. Naomi's breath caught nervously when she saw the two mean-looking girls whisper to each other. Then the taller of the two raised her hand. The teacher nodded for her to come forward and, as she put on her helmet, she looked straight at Naomi with a smile. Naomi's blood ran cold. It was a fake and sinister smile. She could feel it.

Naomi stole a glance at Midori, who was watching uneasily from across the circle of students. Excited, Ai pushed Naomi forward into the ring. Some of the girls in the group applauded. On the other side of the gym, the noise subsided as the boys noticed what was going on. Naomi numbly put on her helmet and stepped forward. The two girls met in the centre and bowed before stepping back to ready themselves for the match. Naomi looked at the eyes behind her opponent's intimidating mask. They were staring back at her, boring holes right through her. To Naomi, the girl looked like Darth Vader.

At the teacher's signal, Naomi moved. With her heart racing, she faced down her opponent.

THWAP!

Naomi reeled in surprise from the force of a solid strike to her chest protector. She thought she could hear a collective gasp, and then a few snickers, from the group. The teacher nodded. It was a good move; one point for the mean-looking girl. Naomi felt a shot of adrenaline rush down her arms and out through her fingertips. Without seeming to think about it, she regained her balance and took a determined step forward towards her opponent.

THWAP!

Again, Naomi felt herself caught off guard. She staggered back a step and looked up at her rival. The teacher shook her head. No point for that blow, but Naomi still felt humiliated. She heard more snickering and knew it was coming from her opponent's friend. Naomi stood still for a moment, trying to put them both out of her mind. It wasn't easy. *Okay, Darth Vader, I get it, now. You mean business.* She forced herself to relax and take a deep breath. Her body and mind balanced together for an extra moment. Then Naomi took two mighty steps forward and lunged, her arms in tune with the rest of her body. She directed her bamboo sword first to her opponent's mid-section and then, without breaking her rhythm, another lunge and a smart, quick strike to the helmet.

Her opponent felt both blows. Unable to react in time for Naomi's second move, she was forced backwards. For a moment, she teetered in the balance before falling awkwardly onto the floor.

The crowd gasped. Naomi could hear a few claps. "*Jozu!*" someone called out. A wave of pride, mingled with gratitude and relief, coursed through her. The score was now one point for each girl.

"Vwery good!" A voice called out, followed by a few stifled giggles. *Who said that?* Naomi wondered. And another shot of adrenaline coursed through her as she recognized the voice: Kenji. Naomi quickly glanced over at her opponent's sidekick, and was pleased to see that the girl was looking more than a little concerned, and had stopped her snickering.

Naomi took another deep breath to steady herself. *I can do this*, she told herself firmly.

THWAP! THWAP!

Naomi's and her opponent's bamboo swords met. They lunged and sparred evenly for almost a minute. Naomi delivered several promising shots, but then the other girl delivered a decisive thrust to Naomi's torso. Naomi toppled to the ground. The match was over. Naomi watched as the two mean-looking girls exchanged pleased looks. Darth Vader offered Naomi a dismissive bow as she lay sprawled on the floor of the gym. Then she retreated to her friend, and they exchanged triumphant, wicked grins. There was little applause from the crowd. Slowly, Naomi got up, her face burning. She didn't want to remove her mask, for fear that everyone would see how humiliated she felt. Naomi was grateful for the sound of the bell, signalling the end of the class.

In the changing room, Naomi and her friends were silent. Naomi was reliving her match with Darth Vader in her mind. *I don't mind losing – but not to her*, she thought sullenly.

"I like kendo. Do you, Naomi-chan?" Kiyoka was obviously trying to change the mood. "Would you like to join the Kendo Club with me? It's on Monday after school," she said.

At the moment, it was the last thing Naomi wanted to do. But then she remembered what Keiko had said about kendo – how it was more about self-control than trying to conquer one's opponent. It might be a nice Japanese alternative to her ballet classes.

Naomi put on a smile and nodded. "Yes, I'd love to join the Kendo Club with you."

A troubled look crossed Midori's face. "I am hoping you will join the English Club with us," she said shyly, adding, "The English Club teacher asked me if you will join and help us."

Naomi was interested. "I'd like that! When is it?"

"Wednesday, after school," Midori replied.

"English Club is not interesting, Naomi-chan. It is very small club. Not interesting students," Ai cut in, frank as always.

Naomi watched with surprised amusement as both Midori and Kiyoka threatened to box Ai's ears.

"If you join our English Club, it will be more fun," Midori assured her, as she dug her fingers into Ai's big arm.

"Sure," Naomi replied. "I'll join the English Club. Why not do both?"

As the four girls left for the next class, Naomi's feelings were a jumble of both happiness and apprehension. *With school here, and these after-school clubs, I won't have time to be lonely now*, she thought. But down the crowded corridor, she could see the two mean-looking girls.

I can't be everyone's best friend, she reminded herself, recalling her mother's words that morning. Right now, though, they seemed a cold comfort. *Why not?* Naomi wanted to ask.

十六

Discovering Sumo

"Moshi-moshi. Naomi desu."

"Hello, Naomi-chan. Are you free today?"

Naomi smiled as she heard Ai's voice over the phone. She was impressed with Ai's attempts to practise her English, knowing that of her three best friends, Ai had the hardest time.

"Yes, Ai-chan, I am free. Do you have an idea?"

"*Eh, to –*" Ai stammered, looking for words. "My brother is five years old. My family – we will go to the shrine. Then, please come to my house."

Naomi was puzzled. *Maybe it's his birthday*, she decided as she checked with her mother and then returned to the phone to reply, "I can come."

"*Yokatta!* We will come to your house at eleven o'clock. Bye-bye," Ai answered back happily.

Sara noticed the puzzled look on Naomi's face. "What is it, Naomi?" she asked, as she poured orange juice into three glasses.

"Ai asked me to go with her family to the shrine today," Naomi answered, then gulped down half the glass of juice. "She said that her brother is five years old. Maybe it's his birthday today – Ai didn't say."

Keiko's eyes twinkled. "I'm sure that today is not his birthday. But it is a special day for him, because he is five years old." With that, Keiko started in on her French toast, waiting for Naomi to take up challenge.

Naomi laughed. "What do you mean? What's so special about today?"

"It is *shichi-go-san*," Keiko replied. "All over Japan, little girls aged three and seven, and boys aged five, will go to the shrines and ask for good luck. Their parents and grandparents will give them presents. It's a special day for them."

"*Shichi – go – san*. Oh, I see: seven, five, three," Naomi said, then giggled. "That's neat," she declared as she speared a forkful of French toast and munched happily. Naomi enjoyed visiting shrines and temples in Pippu-cho. There was one small shrine just down the street, not much larger than a classroom. Sometimes, Naomi would go there just to sit in the small garden to think things through, like when the two mean-looking girls in her class were being especially annoying, or when she wanted to take a break from her home-schooling. If she was feeling lonely for Canada, a visit to the little shrine down the street always cheered her up. She spent a lot of time in the garden thinking about going home to Manitoba for Christmas.

When Naomi and Ai arrived at the big shrine, it was abuzz with children of all sizes, proud parents, and grandparents, just like Keiko said it would be. Even little five-year-old Makoto, Ai's brother, seemed very aware that this was his special day. He walked importantly up the front steps of the shrine, joining other five-year-old boys dressed in traditional ceremonial outfits. He stood straight as a soldier, unsmiling, as his father took his photograph in front of the shrine. Ai laughed, and then grabbed Naomi by the coatsleeve. "Let's go," she said and scampered up the steps to stand beside her little brother. Makoto looked up at his big sister, smiled broadly, and grabbed her hand.

Along the path leading to the shrine, various food and game stalls had been set up. Ai and Naomi walked slowly along the pathway, browsing. Children were lined up for cotton candy, no doubt drawn in by the sweet warm scent that enveloped the area. Others were trying to win prizes in bean-bag tossing games and ring-throwing games. Naomi was surprised by the variety of things for sale: goldfish, baby chicks, brightly coloured pinwheels and spinning tops, delicate paper fans, shocking pink vinyl handbags with the pictures of the cartoon characters so beloved by Japanese school children.

There were at least two hundred lucky little three-, five- and seven-year-olds at the shrine today. The scene was so colourful that Naomi just stood and stared, trying to engrave the colours and sights in her mind.

"*Irrashai, Naomi-chan*," Ai's mother said as they arrived at the doorstep of Ai's home.

"*Irrashai*. Meaning is 'welcome,'" Ai said importantly to Naomi. Ai spoke loudly enough for her mother and father to hear. They looked at each other and nodded approvingly. Naomi smiled; Ai loved to show off her English. She didn't know as many words as Midori or Kiyoka, but she was never afraid to speak up. And if she didn't know, she would simply guess. Only little Makoto was not impressed. He waved his silver helium balloon to remind everyone that today, he was supposed to be the centre of attention.

Ai made a beeline for the television as they entered the house. "*Sumo basho*," she said to Naomi and switched on the set. She motioned to Naomi to join her on the floor by the *kotatsu*. Ai's mother rolled her eyes and smiled at Naomi, then headed to the kitchen.

"Do you like sumo?" Ai asked Naomi. "Sumo is my favourite sport."

Naomi looked at Ai then shrugged. She followed Ai's gaze over to the TV. Her eyes widened. She had never seen such a bizarre sight! Two enormous men were hunched over, facing each other, with their fists pressed to the ground. They wore nothing on their bodies except for a wide belt wrapped many times around their bellies and between their legs. Their black hair was sleeked into ponytails that were, somehow, twisted ornately on top of their heads. Naomi stared at the television in stunned amazement. "No way. What is this?" she asked out loud to no one in particular.

Naomi watched as the enormous men strutted around the ring, eyeing each other fiercely. The arena crowd was enjoying every moment. The two fat men returned to their respective corners, grabbed a hold of some white powder and proceeded to scatter it around the ring in front of them. They slapped their thighs and lumbered about, each trying to psyche out their opponent. An umpire stood and waited for them to come together and face each other in the ring. They hunkered down with one fist planted on the ground, glowering at each other. Then, in an instant, the two huge men lunged forward. Naomi watched, transfixed, as they began pushing at each other with their hands and bodies. They were trying to grab at each other's belts. One wrestler would make headway as the other was forced back a few feet, but then he would regain his balance and gain momentum, forcing the first man to lose his ground. The larger of the two managed to get a hold of the other's belt and then, half lifting and half pushing, he thrust his opponent off the raised platform on which they had been fighting. The loser fell into a row of other half-naked wrestlers seated on the floor by the ring.

"*Ah, yorikiri*," Ai said as she slapped her knee. It was clear to Naomi that Ai was hooked on this sport. Ai looked over at her, laughed, and said, "In Japan, everyone like sumo."

Naomi watched as the losing sumo wrestler hopped back up on the platform to bow to the referee and the winner before jumping down and stalking away to the dressing room. The winner, to much applause from the crowd, squatted in the ring and gestured with his hands, before receiving an envelope from the referee. *What a – crazy – sport this is*, Naomi thought. Immediately, two more sumo wrestlers were ushered into the arena and up onto the platform. They were both large men, but one was shockingly enormous.

"He is Konishiki," Ai said reverentially. "He is the biggest sumo wrestler – 275 kilograms."

Naomi looked at her friend's face, and almost burst into giggles when she realized it reminded her of the look on Lois's face whenever she talked about her favourite boy band. The umpire and the two wrestlers carried out the same ceremonious rituals as before; slapping their thighs and glowering at each other, throwing the white stuff over the ring, crouching down to face each other off, only to get up again and repeat the moves. The tension was building, and the crowd was applauding wildly.

"They throw *shio* – salt. To frighten away bad spirits," Ai explained.

Then they were off. Slapping and heaving their bulk against each other, the two sumo wrestlers pushed each other around the ring. The smaller of the two dodged as the larger wrestler charged. In an instant, the enormous Konishiki was sprawled flat on the ground. Ai gasped. Naomi guessed that this was one of the more embarrassing ways to lose a match.

After five more matches, the tournament ended for the day. "Finished," Ai said, and shut off the television. She turned to Naomi and asked, "What do you think?"

Naomi was speechless.

Ai looked at Naomi, wide-eyed. "Sumo is beautiful, no?"

Naomi giggled. "Beautiful?" she asked. Then she thought of Lois and her scrapbooks of all her favourite boy bands. "Yes, I think so, too."

"So, how was your day with Ai?" asked Sara at dinner that evening.

"The *shichi-go-san* festival was fun. It was so cute to see all those little kids all dressed up for their special day," Naomi replied. Then she broke into a big grin. "But I saw sumo wrestling today." She stopped. In silence, she looked from her mother to Keiko, who began to smile.

Keiko nodded and said, "You must think that sumo is very strange. But sumo wrestlers are some of the most highly regarded people in Japan. Sumo wrestling is one of the most respected traditions of all. It may look like two very fat men trying to push each other around a ring, but it takes a lot of skill."

Naomi nodded slowly, "It does look strange to me. But I think I can understand what you are saying. I wonder what people in Canada would think of it."

"The most famous sumo wrestler of all time is Chiyonofuji. He is retired now," explained Keiko. "But everyone liked him. He was not so big. But he was strong – and handsome. People called him 'the wolf' because he looked like a wolf." Keiko smiled. "Actually, Chiyonofuji comes from Hokkaido. People from Hokkaido are very proud of that."

"Sumo wrestlers are stars in Japan, as famous as any movie star," Keiko continued. "They live together in teams, or stables, we call them. They exercise all day and eat a special kind of food called *chanko nabe*. Of course, they have to eat a lot. They grow their hair long, so that they can wear it in the special style for the tournaments. When they retire, there is a big ceremony, and the hair is cut off. It is a very emotional ceremony." Keiko went on, "In the area of Tokyo where they live, it is not uncommon to see them walking in the street. Even to touch a sumo wrestler brings good luck to us."

Naomi wondered how she could explain sumo wrestling to Baba, Gigi, Imee and Lois back home. She giggled at the thought – they'd have to see it to believe it. She knew they would see sumo wrestling at first as incredibly bizarre – even comical. She realized they would have to know a lot more about Japan for them to really understand what sumo was about.

十七

Never Going Home

Naomi had just closed her math textbook when she heard a car stop in front of the house. She checked her watch. It was only four o'clock. Her mother wouldn't be home for at least another hour. She looked out the window and saw the postman, carrying a large box to the front door. Curious and excited, Naomi quickly put on her house slippers and went downstairs, meeting Keiko at the front door.

The box bore Canadian postage stamps, and her grandmother's familiar handwriting. "It's a package from Baba and Gigi," Naomi cried out excitedly, as Keiko signed the receipt notice. "*Domo arigato*," Naomi said cheerfully as she scooped up the box and set it gently on the table in the kitchen. "I wonder what it is?" she asked out loud, and she picked it up again and hefted it to check its weight. A few things moved gently inside the box. Naomi was itching with curiosity. She ran her fingers over the line of tape that stretched across the top of the box.

Keiko looked from Naomi to the box. "Perhaps you should wait for Sara-san to get home this evening, don't you think?"

"Oh, it's alright. Maybe Baba sent us some warm winter clothes or something," Naomi smiled, trying to decide the best way to open the box. "I'll take it upstairs to my room." She reached her arms around the big box. She couldn't see the concern in Keiko's eyes as she awkwardly made her way up the stairs.

Naomi grabbed her Swiss Army knife and made a clean cut across the top of the box. Her eyes widened in delight as her favourite fluffy winter housecoat practically burst out of the box. "Great!" she said, and scooped it up in her arms. Her lined winter boots were in the box, too, as well as her mother's favourite green suede cowboy boots. As Naomi lifted out the boots, she noticed that underneath, there were several packages wrapped in Christmas paper. She stopped and stared. She could feel a burning sensation in her stomach. All of a sudden, she felt she didn't even want to breathe. Very slowly, she lifted these packages out, and her eye caught something bright. Baba and Gigi had sent tinsel. Naomi grabbed the package of shaggy gold and silver tinsel and threw it across the floor. Christmas lights, and some other decorations were wrapped in plastic underneath. There were packages of food as well: buckwheat, poppyseeds. This was Ukrainian Christmas food! What was going on?

Naomi scrabbled around on the *tatami* floor, rummaging through all the packages. She lunged at an envelope attached to one of the gift-wrapped parcels, tore it open, and began to read:

> *Dear Sara and Naomi,*
> *We are so disappointed that you won't be coming home for Christmas...*

Naomi's face crumpled as she read Baba's familiar handwriting:

> *...we understand that it is expensive to fly...*

"This isn't happening! This isn't happening!" Naomi yelped. The letter shook in her hands:

> *...we'll just have to wait, then. I sent you some things to remind you of home...*

"She said we could go hoooome!" Naomi wailed. Her chest and stomach ached with fury and disbelief. With a violent sweep of her arm, Naomi sent the packages flying. She flopped herself down and buried her head in her favourite housecoat. Her body heaved with uncontrollable sobs. In the kitchen downstairs, Keiko listened with a pained expression, and slowly dialled Sara's number at work.

"Hello, is Sara Nazarevich the English teacher there by any chance?" Keiko asked politely. And then, "Sara-san. The Christmas package from your parents has arrived. Naomi has opened it. She's very upset ..."

"You promised! You lied!" Naomi spat the words out as her mother opened the bedroom door less than an hour later. Sara still had on her winter coat and Naomi could see snow melting on her mother's shoulders and hair.

Naomi's mother sighed wearily, and looked at her daughter uneasily. "Okay. You have the right to be angry. I should have told you sooner –"

"You LIED!" Naomi shouted.

Sara reached for her daughter's arm, trying to calm her down. "Please, keep your voice down, Naomi. I said 'maybe.' And that was a long time ago. I thought you were getting along alright here by now."

"You didn't tell me! Or ASK me!" Naomi hissed, jerking her arm away.

"Because I knew what your answer would be," Sara said wearily. She took off her coat and threw it over the chair, and sat down. Her eyes surveyed the packages strewn across the room, as if noticing them for the first time. They came to rest on the letter that lay next to her daughter. "Look, Naomi. Do you know how much it costs to fly from Hokkaido to Winnipeg – at any time, never mind Christmas?"

"When were you going to tell me?" Naomi cut in fiercely.

Sara leaned forward, resting her elbows on her knees. "I was going to tell you this week, Naomi. Really, I was. But I knew what your reaction would be." Sara looked long and hard at her daughter, who sat on the floor glaring back at her. "And I wasn't wrong," she finished sadly.

Naomi could see the disappointment in her mother's eyes and, for a moment, she felt ashamed. She stared down at the pattern on her winter housecoat. *Wait a minute*, she told herself, *this is not my fault*. Anger surged up again inside her. "You tell me. ASK me!" she barked.

"Stop talking like that!" Sara responded, losing her patience.

"Maybe I got it from you, huh? Maybe I learned it from you and dad," Naomi shot back. Her scalp prickled. *Where did that come from?*

Sara sat up in the chair and looked at her daughter with wide eyes. Neither of them spoke for a long time. Then, finally, she got down on the floor beside her daughter. For a long time, she sat with her hands in her lap. Naomi waited to see what was going to happen next.

"Naomi – I'm sorry," her mother began. "I'm sorry that things haven't worked out well for us, as a family." Naomi saw a tear fall on the back of her mother's hand. "I don't know what else to say about it, Naomi." Sara looked into her daughter's eyes.

Naomi looked at her mother. She didn't know what else to say, either.

"Maybe I should have said something sooner," Sara continued, then chuckled dryly. "I think maybe I should have said something sooner – about a lot of things, honey." She reached out to put a hand on her daughter's shoulder. "I brought you here because it was the best way I could think of to start a life for you and me. To be independent. I realize you haven't had much of a say in it."

Naomi nodded forlornly.

Sara looked at her daughter and a weak smile spread across her lips. "You're almost thirteen years old. You're growing up so fast. Sometimes I look at you and it's so hard to believe that you're not the happy little six-year-old. I just have to face up to it." She paused for a moment, looking for words. "I know that I owe you more of an explanation, Naomi. If you ever want to ask me about your father, what happened between us, why we divorced, I promise I will try to tell you the answers as honestly as I can."

Naomi nodded again, mutely. She hadn't expected any of this. But now that she heard it, it felt good. It felt like it was what she needed to hear. The knot of fear, and anger, and helplessness began to loosen a little. She still wanted to go home for Christmas, but, somehow, in some other way, she felt a little bit better. She looked at her mother's hands and mumbled, "Thanks."

Sara leaned over to hug her daughter. The hug was so strong Naomi almost laughed as she felt her breath being forced out of her lungs, emitting instead an odd hiccup-like sound. Naomi and her mother drew apart to look at each other, giggled, and then hugged each other again.

Naomi sighed. She took a deep breath. Wistfully, she thought of a Manitoba Christmas: hay rides; her Grandmother's cooking; exchanging presents at school; a fat, red-faced Santa. Her thoughts detoured to visions of bright red cheeks on the little girls celebrating *shichi-go-san* day, and of fat sumo wrestlers. Naomi giggled in spite of herself at this thought, and her mother looked at her quizzically.

"I want you to know that my plan wasn't to ignore Christmas," Sara said. "Actually, I wanted to surprise you with a special trip. I've decided that it would be nice to go to Kyushu for Christmas – to the place I used to live before you were born."

Naomi's face brightened a little. Encouraged, Sara added: "I thought we'd stop in Hiroshima on the way. We could visit the Hiroshima Peace Park." Naomi knew about Hiroshima, the Japanese city where the atomic bomb was dropped during World War Two.

Sara continued, "I asked mom and dad to send this stuff for a reason, Naomi. I have an idea. When I lived in Kyushu, I put on a Christmas party for my colleagues at my junior-high school. Your dad even dressed up as Santa. Back then, some of my friends had never seen a real live Santa before! Keiko-san helped me get a tree ..."

A Christmas party for my friends here would be fun, Naomi thought. She would have a chance to show Kiyoka, Midori, and Ai what a real Ukrainian-Canadian Christmas was all about. Her mind began to race with ideas. *I'll invite everyone from the English Club as well,* she thought, becoming increasingly excited by the idea. *It's going to be a lot of work, but I can do it!*

Later that night, lying on her futon, Naomi again found herself thinking about hay rides with her friends, and Billy romping in the snow, and Baba cooking happily in the kitchen making Christmas goodies. *All these things I won't be seeing this Christmas,* she thought mournfully. Tears began to sting her eyes. She pulled her little notebook out from its secret hiding place under her desk, and began to write:

> *Dear Diary,*
> *I wanted to go home so much! It hurt to see the Christmas decorations and letter from Baba. I was angry.*
> *I'm still angry about it. Why do I just have to live with other people's decisions? It's like I have no power over my own life! But at least I have something to take my mind off it. I will make a Ukrainian-Canadian Christmas party for my friends here. I am learning a lot about Japanese festivals and I would like my friends here to know something about my life, too.*

I wish I could go home for Christmas, but I know Canada (and Christmas) will still be there when I get back.

PS When you think something's going to happen, and it doesn't, it's always good to have a back-up plan.

十八

A Ukrainian-Canadian-Japanese Christmas Party

Naomi, Sara, Keiko and Midori – who had come over early to help – were still running around the house putting on the final touches in preparation for the big event when the doorbell rang. Naomi felt a momentary feeling of panic and could see that Midori, too, was nervous. They peeked out the front window. Seven boys and girls from the English Club, including Kiyoka and Ai, were assembled on the front steps, each holding a small gift box.

"It looks like they're all here – Ai, too!" Naomi said as she smiled at Midori. They both ran to the front door.

"Merry Christmas!" they called out, and opened the door wide. Naomi giggled as she sensed the nervousness in some of them. "Socks are okay – we don't have enough slippers," she said, and everyone laughed as they followed her into the living room. An enormous undecorated pine tree took up the whole corner of the room. There were small presents underneath the tree, as well as the box of decorations from Baba and Gigi. Next to the box were two large metal bowls filled with popcorn and cranberries.

"We're going to celebrate Canadian Christmas Eve," said Naomi proudly. "And a Ukrainian-Canadian Christmas dinner, too – although we don't celebrate Ukrainian Christmas until January," she added. The English Club nodded, impressed and excited. Over the last three weeks, Naomi had been preparing for this day. She had asked the teacher in charge of the English Club if they could focus on a Christmas theme and the teacher had readily agreed. Naomi had talked about Ukrainian as well as Canadian Christmas customs. She taught the English Club members some carols and together they read "The Night before Christmas." At the last English Club meeting, Naomi had passed out invitations to everyone, and was both relieved and grateful to see just how thrilled everyone was. She smiled, remembering the day Ai walked into the English Club meeting and said she wanted to join.

Midori, Kiyoka and Ai, acting as assistant hosts, motioned for the others to put their gifts under the tree and to sit in a circle on the *tatami* floor. Then they handed out string and a needle to each member. Naomi put on some Christmas carols, then sat in the middle of the circle. She knotted the end of her string and threaded her needle. "Take some popcorn, and some cranberries, like this," she explained, as she carefully strung some of each on her string. In no time, everyone was busy stringing ropes of red and white.

Sara came from the kitchen carrying a large punchbowl, followed by Ai with a tray of glasses, which they placed on the table by the front window. "This is eggnog. It's a special Christmas drink," Naomi explained as she began ladling the drink into the glasses.

"*Oishii desu,*" Naomi heard someone say.

"English only!" said someone else.

"Let's decorate the Christmas tree now," Naomi suggested. Coloured Christmas lights were strung up first. The popcorn and cranberry strings were tied into one long piece and wrapped carefully around the large pine. Naomi passed the box of ornaments and tinsel around and each member took turns to hang a few pieces. She giggled as she watched them debate where to hang each piece. Then she went to the kitchen to get her mother and Keiko, before turning off the living room lights. In the darkened room, she passed out song sheets and said, "Let's light up the tree and sing 'Oh Christmas Tree.' Who would like to light up the tree?" A small boy with a cheeky grin stepped forward quickly, and flicked on the switch. In the darkness, the Christmas tree burst into points of green, red, yellow and blue light. The group cheered and clapped.

After singing the carol, everyone continued to admire the tree. Naomi was amazed to learn that most of her guests had never had a

Christmas tree of their own. Midori and Kiyoka went to help Keiko and Sara in the room next door, and soon everyone began to smell the delicious and exotic aromas from the food that Naomi and her mother had spent so long to prepare. After peeking into the room to check that everything was ready, Naomi pushed aside the screen door separating the living room from the formal dining room. A linen tablecloth had been spread across two *kotatsu*, one of which Takenaka-sensei had lent for the occasion. An array of delicious-looking foods covered the makeshift banquet table. "This is a traditional Ukrainian Christmas dinner," Naomi explained proudly, "which Keiko-san and my mother helped to make."

The students looked around the table for their name cards, which Naomi had made with coloured paper in the shape of yule logs, Christmas boxes, reindeer, and snowflakes. When they all had found their places, Naomi began to explain each dish. "At Ukrainian Christmas, it is the custom to eat twelve meatless dishes."

"*Niku nashi* – No meat," Ai cut in, by way of translation.

Naomi smiled at her friend, and pointed to a dish next to her. Enunciating carefully, she said, "We have *pampushky* – sweet buns. *Hryby* – mushrooms. *Kvacolia* – beans. *Holubtsi* – cabbage rolls – "

The boys and girls seated around the table began to giggle as Naomi spoke the odd-sounding Ukrainian words. "Horab-shichi?" pronounced Takeshi, a tall boy from the eighth grade.

"Ho-dab-chi!" exclaimed a petite, pretty girl that Naomi knew only from the English Club, though they would often exchange shy smiles when they passed each other in the corridors at school.

Naomi giggled as they tried to get their tongues around the strange new language. She then pointed to a beautiful golden-brown loaf of bread, made in the shape of a braid. "This is *kalach*. And this," she continued, pointing to a large tureen filled with a purple soup, "is called *borscht*." Everyone laughed at the sound of that word, and Naomi laughed along with them, shaking her head. She pointed next to a large platter right in the centre of the large table. "And these are my favourite – we call them *perogies*. You'll love them." She looked hungrily at the huge plate of steaming boiled perogies.

"Looks like *gyoza*," a boy named Hajime observed, referring to the boiled meat-filled dumplings that originate from China and are a popular snack food all over Japan.

"I think so, too," Naomi nodded. She pointed to a bowl of stewed fruit and said, "This is *uzvar*, a fruit compote."

Ai and another girl leaned forward to smell the fish. "Delicious," they declared in unison.

"That's *ruba*," Naomi explained. She waved her hand over the remaining dishes and then lifted the lid off another large tureen. Everyone craned their necks to see what was inside. They exchanged quizzical glances at each other, not sure what to make of the thick grey mixture flecked with bits of black. Naomi smiled at their expressions and explained. "This is *kutia*. It is made of wheat, honey, and poppyseeds. You'll love it," she assured her friends. "Okay. Merry Christmas, everybody. Let's eat."

The group proceeded to help themselves from the various platters. The boys seemed to be less bashful at the table, but even the girls were heaping food on their plates; the lovely aromas had whetted their appetites. They helped themselves to seconds. Some boys ate even more after that. One by one, the English Club members sat back from the table, grinning contentedly.

"*Gochisosama deshita*," they said one after another.

Naomi surveyed the table filled with empty plates and serving dishes and was surprised herself at how well they had managed to tuck into the Ukrainian Christmas feast. She looked around at everyone and grinned. "We're not finished yet," she declared.

People were holding their stomachs and groaning good-naturedly.

"We have an important custom to do," Naomi began, grinning mischievously. "After dinner, we throw some of the *kutia* on the ceiling," she said, gesturing the action. Naomi looked around the table at the confused faces. But Ai dipped a spoon in the tureen of *kutia* and ceremoniously handed it to her, Japanese-style; with both hands, a solemn bow – and a twinkle in her eye.

Naomi accepted the spoon with equal solemnity, and almost laughed out loud. "We fling a little *kutia* to the ceiling. If most of it sticks, then we know we will have a good harvest."

Everyone looked nervous as Naomi tested the weight of the kutia and looked up at the ceiling. "Don't worry – Keiko-san said no problem. And I'll clean it up later." She stood up and raised the spoonful of *kutia* over her shoulder. She quickly snapped her arm forward. The dollop of *kutia* hit the ceiling of Keiko's house and splattered in a small line. The English Club held its collective breath – the *kutia* stuck fast!

Naomi looked across at everyone seated, grinned and bowed. "This is the Japan-Canada Kutia Summit Meeting," she began authoritatively, "And I can say that the harvest will be good."

"Great!" some exclaimed, laughing, as they clapped their hands.

"Now let's open our presents," Naomi said. The children rose from the table and seated themselves around the decorated Christmas tree, glittering brightly in the cozy living room. All of the English Club members looked with anticipation at the gifts they had brought, now placed under the tree. They were expecting to begin exchanging presents with each other, having picked names out of a hat at the last English Club meeting. Instead, Naomi pulled a big bag out from behind the tree and began passing small packages to each boy and girl. "Go ahead, open them," she urged. Within seconds, wrapping paper had been torn away and all of the members were holding up pairs of red and green striped Christmas socks with reindeer faces all over them. Everyone laughed as Naomi opened her own little package and proceeded to put on her socks, with Ai, Kiyoka, and Midori eagerly following her example. The tall boy rolled up his pants and stuck out his legs for full effect, to guffaws of laughter all around.

"Okay everyone, let's line up and get a group shot," Naomi said, passing a camera to her mother and scampering over to the group as they stood in front of the tree.

"You guys look too posed," Sara said, assessing the group. "Do the 'hokey pokey' and put your right foot in."

The English Club laughed at those familiar words and everyone stuck their right foot into a semi-circle, showing off their new Christmas socks. Those wearing pants happily pulled up their pant legs to show the goofy-looking stripes with the reindeer heads. Everyone stuck their other hand out, fingers extended in the "V" sign, and said "cheese" as Sara took the photograph. From somewhere in the house, the faint sound of sleighbells could be heard.

"Ah, Jingle Bells?" asked one of the English Club members.

The jingling sound became louder and louder as everyone, including Naomi, looked at each other. Wide-eyed, Naomi stared at her mother and then Keiko, who returned her puzzled look with enigmatic expressions. The sound appeared to come from the next room, and then Santa appeared from around the corner! Everyone gaped as Santa, dressed in his red velvet suit with white fake-fur trim and black socks, entered the room, ringing some sleigh bells. His face was completely covered by a full white beard and the bushiest white eyebrows Naomi had ever seen.

"Ho ho ho ho, Merry Christmas. Ho ho ho. Rudolph is outside, so I can't stay long." He took a seat in the large armchair beside the Christmas tree and reached for the nearest gift box, bringing it close to his face in order to read the name on the tag. "This is for Yurie Goto," Santa called out. Yurie stood up and timidly walked over to Santa, who asked, "Have you been a good girl this year?" The girl smiled shyly, not knowing what to say. Sara snapped a photo before Santa called out the next recipient, Ai, who boldly decided to sit on Santa's lap, and smiled brightly for the camera.

Midori had the strangest expression on her face when her turn came to collect her Christmas present, for by now, both she and Naomi had realized the identity of the mysterious Santa. After one more group photograph and a few more Christmas carols, it was time for Santa to leave. "I must be going, I have a lot of Christmas presents to deliver down in Tokyo. Merry Christmas, everyone. And keep up your English!" Santa couldn't help but finish on an academic note, and Naomi, Midori, Keiko and Sara looked at each other, trying hard to suppress giggles. Naomi looked around the room. Everyone was thrilled to have met Santa, whoever he was. She was grateful that the English Club Christmas party had been a success ... and especially for her surprise Japanese Santa. She looked across the room at Ai, who was staring at her indignantly, hands on hips, as if to say: You're keeping secrets from me!

Naomi went over to her friend, grabbed two treats out of the bowl on the table, and waved one in front of Ai. "Candy cane?" she asked.

Ai grabbed the candy from Naomi. "Tell me who!" she said. But Naomi just took a loud, crunching bite off the end of her cane, eyes dancing behind a smile that couldn't stay hidden any longer.

十九

One Thousand Cranes

"I'm glad we decided to take the train, mom."

"Me, too," Sara replied. "It's too bad you don't get much of a chance to use the train on the prairies. I think it's the best way. You can see how the landscape – even the climate – is changing, as we head south."

Naomi nodded and gazed out the window of the train. While Hokkaido had been blanketed by a thick layer of snow, somewhere between Aomori and Sendai, the snow had begun to thin out. She pulled a pencil and her diary out of her rucksack and began to write:

> *snow blankets the fields*
> *a crow is circling above*
> *hungry and lonely*

Naomi read the poem to herself, with a satisfied nod. "This one I'm going to send to the *haiku* contest." She had already sent in three *haiku* poems since Takenaka-sensei put out the challenge to her and Midori, but she had had no luck yet. Each week, Naomi eagerly looked for the winning entry and read it with interest. Naomi and Midori would often share their poems and critique each other's work.

Naomi and her mother were headed to the southern island of Kyushu to spend the Christmas holidays. They were going to the place where Sara had worked as a university graduate and where she had met Keiko more than fourteen years before, right at the opposite end of Japan from Hokkaido. Naomi and her mother had been on the trains for more than a day, now. Even so, Naomi never tired of looking out the window. With a rucksack of books to read, as well as her diary and a small sketch book, she wasn't bored at all.

Just that morning, she and her mother had arrived in Tokyo. Sara had whisked her daughter off for a whirlwind tour of the sprawling city. Naomi found herself rubbing her neck, which had become a little stiff. It seemed to her that she had spent the entire time in Tokyo looking up to the sky; at all the tall buildings, at the ornate roofs of some of the loveliest temples and shrines she had ever seen. It was as if the life of this incredible city didn't happen on the street but existed "up there;" entire highways were not at ground level but up in the air, winding through Tokyo like giant snakes; roads were even built over the river that flowed through the city. At intersections, people crossed the streets on elevated pedestrian walkways. Naomi just couldn't believe the swarm of electronics shops in Akihabara, the crowded sidewalks which brought them both to a standstill, and all the skyscrapers of the bustling Shinjuku district. The barrage of signs, in English as well as Japanese, was unlike anything in Portage la Prairie – or Winnipeg, for that matter. Naomi stuck close to her mother the whole time. She was more than a little relieved when her mother took her to the famous Yoyogi Park, where they enjoyed a quiet stroll among trees and through a peaceful shrine before catching the train to Hiroshima.

Now, as the *shinkansen* super-high-speed bullet train made its way south, Naomi sat back in her chair, gazing in awe at the massive urban sprawl all around her. They had been on the train for over an hour and weren't in Tokyo anymore. Yet, for all she knew, she was still in that same enormous city. As far as she could see, there was nothing but office buildings, apartment blocks, streets, billboards, houses, stores, freeways and traffic. She turned to look out the window on the left side of the train, and saw the same thing. Naomi noticed tall green netted structures which Sara explained were either golf driving ranges or baseball batting cages. Both sports were especially popular in Japan.

Naomi smiled, recalling the names of some of Japan's top baseball teams. The best-loved team by far was the Yomiuri Giants. But there were also the Kintetsu Buffaloes, the Yakult Swallows, the Chunichi Dragons and the Hiroshima Carps. There was even a team called the Nippon Ham Fighters! Suddenly, Winnipeg Goldeyes didn't seem like such a funny name for a baseball team.

Then her thoughts turned to the city of Hiroshima, where she and her mother would arrive in just a few hours. Surely everyone in Canada knew about this place, made famous – or infamous – as the city where the first atomic bomb was dropped during World War Two. Naomi pictured in her mind the image of a city wiped out by the nuclear blast; miles of rubble and, in the middle, the rounded dome of virtually the only building left standing after the attack. This was now the Hiroshima Peace Park, and she and her mother would be there, soon.

Naomi pulled a book from her rucksack and studied the cover. It was a drawing of a young girl. In the background was a collection of folded paper cranes. She gazed at the title, *Sadako and the Thousand Paper Cranes*, for a few moments, and then opened the book. It was the story of a young athletic girl who was twelve years old at the time of the atomic bomb blast in Hiroshima. Sadako survived the blast but, when she was fourteen, she developed leukemia, a cancer of the blood that many believe was due to the nuclear fallout from the bomb. In Japanese lore, it is believed that if a person is ill, they can be cured by folding one thousand paper cranes. Sadako began to fold paper cranes. Over time, people heard her story and began to help her. Naomi was soon engrossed in the story of Sadako.

"Look! Naomi!" She was jolted by her mother's excited voice. Naomi looked up at her mother, then out the window. She gasped.

There was Mount Fuji – one of the most famous mountains in the world – right in front of her! It was as if the window of the train was one big picture postcard. Mount Fuji stood out against the deep blue of the sky, majestic and apart from its surroundings, like a sentinel. Naomi and her mother looked in silence as the mountain moved across the window of the bullet train.

"We're lucky it's December. The best views are in winter," Sara said.

"It looks so – perfect," Naomi replied. She noticed that the green countryside had returned, with a smattering of snow on the ground, and a wide band of snow high on Mount Fuji. Somewhere along the way, the grey urban sprawl had ended, but Naomi, engrossed in the story of Sadako, hadn't even noticed.

"...box lunches, coffee, tea, ice cream..." Naomi heard the high-pitched female voice intone in Japanese. It was a voice which had, by now, become quite familiar to Naomi. The uniformed girl came, pushing the cart laden with drinks, plastic boxes of food and snacks of all kinds.

Naomi's mother bought two lunchboxes and passed one to her. "A *bento* box on a train is not my favourite food in the world, but we'd better have a bite. We still have a way to go before we get to Hiroshima."

Naomi nodded as she lifted the lid off her box. Inside were small compartments, each one holding its own unique little morsel of food. The biggest compartment contained the standard mound of plain white rice, topped with a red pickled plum in imitation of the flag of Japan. There was also a piece of pumpkin boiled in soy sauce and sugar. *That's good*, Naomi thought. Some marinated fish on a piece of dried seaweed. *So far so good*, she mused. Naomi looked at something indescribable and figured it was some sort of seafood. She would pass on that. Next to the rice was some grilled chicken. "Well, mom, it doesn't look bad – just one piece of mystery meat," she said as she pulled the paper wrapper off the disposable wooden chopsticks and pried the two sticks apart. "Mom, we really should start carrying our own chopsticks instead of using these disposable ones. I learned at school that we cut down a lot of trees to make these things," she added, before digging hungrily into her mound of rice. Sara regarded her daughter thoughtfully for a few moments before unwrapping her own chopsticks.

The train stopped in Kyoto for four minutes. "Big Japanese cities look the same," Naomi remarked, as she looked out onto the platform.

Sara laughed, "I don't blame you for thinking so. From the train station, they really do all look the same; the same chain restaurants, parking lots, and row after row of bicycles. But Kyoto is special. I wish we had time to stay." She looked down at Naomi. "We'll come back someday – if you want to."

"That's okay, mom. I'm looking forward to Hiroshima. I'm enjoying the book about Sadako and the thousand cranes." Naomi said as she showed her mother the book. She was almost half-way through the story.

"I love that story, too," Sara replied. She gave her daughter a hug as the train pulled out of the station and began to pick up speed.

"Hiroshima. This is Hiroshima. Please don't leave anything behind," the conductor's voice drawled as the train came to a smooth stop about two hours later.

"I can still feel myself moving," said Naomi. She was standing still on the platform beside the train, with her arms stretched out before her, as if to steady herself.

Her mother laughed. "The bullet train does that to you. We were going at three hundred kilometres per hour. Do you realize that you've never travelled that fast – and still been on land?" she asked. Naomi nodded, impressed.

Within half an hour, she and her mother were standing in Hiroshima Peace Park, gazing up at a bronze statue. The bottom was a large obelisk-like structure, tall enough for people to walk under. On top of this base was the statue of a young girl. She was holding out her arms. Above the girl was the delicate frame of a folded paper crane. The outstretched arms of the girl and the wings of the crane were joined. Naomi gazed up at the statue of the young girl, Sadako, and a strange feeling came over her. She couldn't understand exactly what she was feeling. It was like flight and freedom, and a lump in her throat, all mixed together. Naomi hadn't yet finished reading the story of Sadako. She looked into the face of this bronze girl, and wondered.

Surrounding the base of the statue were masses of colourful paper cranes, strung together in big bundles of one thousand. These paper cranes were a mountain of colours, shapes, and sizes. Naomi noticed that many of the cranes at the very bottom of the pile were faded from being in the sun and rain for a long time.

"Look, Naomi – these cranes are made by children and sent here from all over the world," Sara said, holding a card attached to one of the bundles. "These are from Finland."

Naomi reached for a tag, and read: *Dear Sadako, Peace on Earth. From the students of Blakehill First School, Bradford, West Yorkshire, England.* She circled the statue, marvelling at the places she discovered: Kwangju, South Korea; Amman, Jordan; Kiev, Ukraine. Naomi wasn't even sure she knew where some of these places were! All these children had joined together in a symbol of peace, to help Sadako get her wish. All of a sudden, Naomi needed to know what had happened to the young girl from Hiroshima.

"Mom, did Sadako get to one thousand cranes?" Naomi asked. She was really asking if the story had a happy ending but, in her heart, she felt she already knew the answer.

Sara looked down at her daughter and put a comforting arm around her shoulders. Together, they looked up at the bronze statue of the girl. "Don't you think, Naomi, how wonderful it is that we – all of us – know about Sadako and her story?" Sara asked.

Naomi looked from her mother to the statue of Sadako. That funny feeling returned to her again, and she nodded.

Christmas in Kyushu

"Wake up, Naomi. It's seven o'clock. The ferry has been sitting here in Beppu for at least an hour." Sara gently shook her daughter awake. The night before, they had boarded the ferry that brought them straight from Hiroshima to the popular hot springs resort city of Beppu, on the island of Kyushu.

Naomi sat up on her elbows and looked around. She was the last person to wake up! Everyone else had already rolled up their blankets and were seated on the floor in small groups. Some were eating breakfast, picnic-style. Naomi thought back to the night before, when they had boarded the ferry in Hiroshima. Her mother had explained that everyone would simply roll out a blanket on the *tatami* floor, marking out their territory for the night. Naomi had to admit she was a little shocked at the idea of spending the night with a hundred strangers, lying side by side in one enormous *tatami* room. "It's not so bad, Naomi," her mother had assured her. "It can be quite interesting. This ferry's not so crowded, anyway."

Naomi got up and went out on deck. The city of Beppu was laid out in front of her. Unlike on the flat prairie, you could actually see the entire city; it stretched along the coast on each side and up at the back, where it was bounded by a row of high hills. Her eyebrow shot up when she spotted a few palm trees. There was a bracing wind up on the deck of the ferry. It felt good after the uncomfortable sleep in the overheated *tatami* room.

Naomi hadn't slept well; she had lain awake for hours, her mind spinning from the visit to the Peace Park, the museum, and the memorial cenotaph. She turned her face to the wind, reflecting on the terrible things she had learned, and seen. She remembered that the bomber pilot had named his plane "Enola Gay," after his mother. And how, upon watching the Earth erupt behind him as he flew out of harm's way – perhaps only then beginning to realize the horror of his mission – he had written in his journal, "My God, what have we done?"

Naomi shuddered as she recalled the exhibits in the museum showing the bomb's devastating effects: glass bottles melted into grotesque shapes by the heat of the nuclear blast, tin plates crumpled like sheets of paper, steel food cans melted in one solid, charred lump, a stack of needles fused together, the head of a stone Buddha statue with its face melted off. There was a display of old watches all reading 8:15, the exact moment when the atomic bomb had struck the city. Huge steel building frames had been bent as if they were toys.

One display had made Naomi's blood run cold. It was the stone steps leading to the entrance of a bank, one-eighth of a mile from the epicentre of the bomb blast. On the steps, Naomi could see a shape: the outline of a man. At 8:15 in the morning on August 6, 1945, the man had been sitting on those steps, waiting for the bank to open. When the bomb fell from the sky, the temperature rose to seven thousand degrees Fahrenheit, burning everything – including people – to nothing. In that one instant, the heat from the blast changed the surface of the stones around the man; stones which now forever held his shadow.

Further from the epicentre, people and animals survived, but with horrible burns. Naomi looked in disbelief at photos of children showing burn marks on their bodies which matched the traditional patterns on the cotton kimono they had been wearing at the time. Many would die later from the effects of radiation.

Over all, she had learned, approximately 200,000 people died as a result of that bomb. And just three days later, another would fall on Nagasaki.

Naomi had been warned by her mother that the museum exhibits were disturbing, but she had wanted to go in. And now, she knew, the horror of nuclear warfare would always be with her. Afterwards, they had visited the cenotaph. Naomi had engraved its words in her mind like a prayer: Repose ye in peace, for the error shall not be repeated.

"Naomi, are you ready? Let's get off this boat. I told Junko that we would take the train all the way to Shonai so she won't have to drive into Beppu." Sara's voice cut in on Naomi's thoughts. She handed Naomi her duffel bag. "I can hardly wait. It's hard to believe that it's been more than a dozen years since I was last here."

Naomi and her mother took the ten-minute train ride to Oita City, which lay hidden from view up the coast, on the other side of Mount Takasaki. There, they switched trains to the Kyudai line, which headed inland along the Yufu River, into the heart of the island of Kyushu. Naomi laughed as she took a seat on the train; it was a small and rickety old thing, so unlike the luxurious bullet train. She felt comforted by the rustic-looking little villages along the way with their wooden picket fences and little streams. The rice fields, so much more abundant here than in Pippu-cho, lay barren, waiting for spring. Small temples and shrines dotted the hillsides. *It looks like a very small-town kind of place – just like where I come from. I can see why mom loved it so much*, she thought.

After half an hour, the train stopped at Shonai station. The station itself was nothing more than a small building, not much larger than a house, made of wood bleached grey over the years. "Are we here?" Naomi asked.

"We're here," her mother replied excitedly. They walked through the small station and onto the street.

A young woman parked her car nearby and quickly emerged, running up to Sara with outstretched arms. It was Junko, Sara's colleague from her time as an English teacher at Hasama Junior-High School.

For the next few days, Junko took Naomi and her mother around the area. They visited the small hot springs village of Yunohira. They took long walks in the hills and through forests. They hiked up small snowy mountains and had picnics at the top, looking out over the small valley below. Sara and Junko showed Naomi the junior-high school where her mother and Keiko had taught together, and drove by the pear farm that had once belonged to Keiko and her husband. Naomi could see why her mother had such fond memories of her time in Japan. The area was incredibly beautiful.

On Christmas Day, after a long goodbye with Junko in Shonai,

Naomi and her mother travelled on to the quaint mountain village of Yufuin, further up the Yufu River towards the heart of Kyushu. They checked into a *minshuku* – a traditional Japanese inn. It was built of thick wooden beams, like a barn, and looked as if it were several hundred years old. Naomi and her mother checked out their little *tatami* room, small but cosy with thick futons rolled up in the corner. The little window looked out onto a grove of pines, and had a view of the town's pride and joy – Mount Yufu.

"Naomi, this place has a *rotemburo*. Let's go find it," Sara said eagerly, as Naomi bounced up and down on the rolled-up pile of futons.

"What's a *rotemburo*?" Naomi asked.

"An outdoor hot spring bath," Sara replied.

"But I didn't bring my bathing suit," Naomi said, disappointed.

Her mother laughed. "This is Japan, you don't need one."

Naomi watched as her mother grabbed the blue and white cotton robes hanging on the door and headed out in search of the inn's traditional bath house. They noticed a grey wooden lean-to across the garden, and headed there. There were two doors to the lean-to; one labelled with the Chinese character for man, the other for woman. Naomi and her mother opened the door marked "woman" and found themselves in a little change room lined with small plastic trays on wooden shelves. A pile of fluffy white towels was in the corner.

Sara opened a second, smaller door, that opened into the bath area. "Coast is clear – nobody here," she whispered. Naomi stood as her mother began to undress. She felt a little embarrassed, but began to undress herself with awkward, modest moves. They wrapped towels around themselves and then opened the door leading to the hot spring bath. Along one wall were several taps and short plastic stools. By each tap lay a bar of soap and small plastic buckets. Sara sat on one of the stools and quickly washed and rinsed herself in the Japanese way, and Naomi followed suit. Then they scampered naked into the hot bath, which opened out away from the lean-to. The hot spring bath was surrounded on one end by the wall with the row of taps, and a wooden wall which jutted out into the pool, dividing it in half. The other two sides were exposed to the outside elements. Naomi bent down low in the water and shuffled out to the far edge of the pool, bordered by a hedge of pine trees.

"What's on the other side of this wall, mom?" Naomi asked as she waded out.

"That's the men's side, Naomi – "

"What!" Naomi shrieked. She did a U-turn and waddled back towards the sheltered part of the pool, safely behind the dividing wooden wall.

Sara laughed. "Don't worry, Naomi. No one's here."

"Yet!" Naomi countered

"True," Sara replied. "But relax. Public bathing is a part of life in Japan. No one will cross over to this side. It's bad manners," she explained. "It was weird for me at first, too. But believe me, you'd look a lot more strange if you came in here wearing a bathing suit."

Naomi was surprised to find that the bath was outdoors, among the rocks and trees. But her surprise soon changed to delight. It was a lovely place. They sat on some rocks in the pool, crouching down so the hot water rose to their chins. Naomi looked across at the pine trees, the mountains beyond and took in a deep breath. Snowflakes began to fall in the twilight. The flakes grew bigger and fluffier, melting as they hit their flushed pink skin. Large grapefruit, called *yuzu*, bobbed in the pool around them.

When they felt they would melt from the heat, Naomi and her mother carefully waded back in towards the lean-to, and grabbed their *yukata*. Giggling, they scampered back to their room before the cold winter chill could rob them of the heat from the hot spring bath.

Naomi put on her pyjamas, and her blue and white robe over top. Then she and her mother wandered into the dining room. It was a small room with a large fireplace at one end. Several other guests, also dressed in their special robes, were already enjoying their meals. They nodded and smiled at Naomi and her mother. It was a warm and cosy place. The waitress brought them the set menu of *miso* soup, a bowl of steaming chicken and rice, and hot green tea.

"I'm starved," Naomi said. "That outdoor hot spring bath was fun, mom. It felt great! But I'm glad we were there by ourselves."

Sara laughed, "I know what you mean. But I have to say that when I left Japan, the thing I missed the most were the hot spring baths – especially the outdoor ones. I always said that I'd like to have a Jacuzzi in my house, in a place where you could open the doors wide ..." her voice trailed off. She looked across at her daughter and smiled a small smile. "Someday."

After dinner, Naomi and her mother snuggled into their futons for the night. It was only 9:30, but Naomi was ready for sleep. With a grin, Sara handed Naomi a present wrapped in Christmas paper. Naomi took a look at the gift and grinned back. With a twinkle in her eye, she reached into her duffel bag and pulled out a small gift-wrapped package.

"Naomi, what a surprise! I didn't think you would have brought something all the way down here — at least, not without mentioning it," Sara said, delighted.

"It wasn't easy, I admit. Here, open it," Naomi thrust the package eagerly at her mother. "Keiko helped me pick it out."

Sara unwrapped her Christmas present — a paperback book called *The River Ki*, by Sawako Ariyoshi. Her eyes widened in delight, and she reached out to hug Naomi. "Thanks so much. It's a lovely gift. She is one of my favourite authors."

Naomi's present was a small red and black lacquer *bento* box with matching chopsticks in its own carrying case. She gave her mother a hug and said, "No more disposable chopsticks! Save the trees! Thanks, mom."

Naomi admired her gift for a few moments, then snuggled down into her futon. They would head back up north in just a few more days. The Christmas holiday was almost over. She rolled over to face her mother, who was already absorbed in the book that Naomi had just given her.

"Mom?"

"Hmmm?"

"I like Japan," Naomi said.

"I'm glad. Me too," Sara replied, as she continued reading.

"Mom — I really like Japan. And I'm sorry for giving you a hard time before about not going back to Manitoba for Christmas."

Sara put down her novel and faced her daughter. "Naomi, it means a lot to me to hear you say that. And I'm glad you liked your Christmas here in Kyushu. This place is an important part of my life." She paused thoughtfully before continuing. "After all, I met your father here. And if I hadn't, I never would've met you."

"Well, it's a good thing you came here, then, mom," Naomi replied with a mock frown.

"It sure is," Sara replied. Her eyes sparkled as she reached over to kiss Naomi's forehead. "Good night, my daughter."

Naomi lay awake and reflected on the Christmas holiday. How different it had been from all her previous Christmases! She sat up in bed, dug a postcard out of her bag next to her, and began to write:

> *Dear Keiko-san,*
> *We've had a fantastic holiday so far! Spent a morning in Tokyo, and an afternoon in Hiroshima. I saw the statue of Sadako there! We had a great time in Shonai and I saw your old pear farm! We went swimming in an outdoor hot spring bath in Yufuin. It's beautiful. Wish you were here. Merry Christmas and Happy New Year!*
> *See you soon.*
> *Love, Naomi (and mom)*

All of these visions danced in Naomi's head as she drifted into a deep sleep.

twenty-one

New Year's Namahage

"Mom, what are we going to do for New Year's Eve?" Naomi asked. Mother and daughter were eating *dango jiru*, a thick vegetable and noodle stew, by the open fire at the inn.

"We're going to Akita-ken, in the northern end of Honshu Island, for a couple of days. It's on the way home, for one thing," Sara explained, grinning, "and Keiko-san will meet us there."

"What? Wow! Oh mom, that's great," Naomi yelped, almost upsetting her bowl of stew. "I was missing her."

"Me, too," Sara replied. She paused a moment before adding, "It's good to be with family at this time of year, if you can."

"Yeah. Keiko-san is like family," Naomi replied thoughtfully.

Sara brightened, "Yes, Keiko-san is family, too."

"I have family all over the world, now," Naomi said matter-of-factly, as she turned her attention back to the bowl in front of her. Sara watched as Naomi grappled with an especially slippery noodle, and felt grateful.

Two days later, after a flight from Oita City to Tokyo and then on to Akita, Sara and Naomi were waiting at the train station. Naomi spotted her first, as she emerged through the turnstiles among a large group of passengers. "Keiko-san!" Naomi cried out happily. She ran to Keiko and reached for her small suitcase. "Welcome to Akita," she said, breathless. Keiko took Naomi's arm and smiled warmly.

"You must be tired, Keiko-san," Sara said, smiling. "We're staying at a *minshuku* – Naomi likes them better than hotels. We'll go there, now."

Keiko-san smiled back, her eyes bright and mischievous. "I like them better, also. It's much more fun to sleep on the floor. Don't you think, Naomi-chan?"

Naomi nodded, then said slyly, "I wonder what Baba and Gigi will think when I go home and ask if I can take my bed apart and put it in storage in the barn?"

"We'll discuss that later," her mother said, and grimaced playfully.

"I'm glad that you came all the way here to spend New Year's Eve with us, Keiko-san," Naomi said.

"I wouldn't want to miss it. It's good for me to get out once in a while. New Year's Eve has been a quiet day for me for a long time – too long," she added thoughtfully. "For the last few years, I would simply do the usual New Year's housecleaning."

Keiko laughed at the confused expression on Naomi's face, and explained, "In Japan, families clean their homes on December 31st. It's a New Year's custom."

"It doesn't sound like a very fun custom," Naomi declared.

Keiko gave Naomi a gentle squeeze around the shoulders as the taxi turned into the small inn. A young girl, the owner's daughter, took them upstairs and showed them to their room. It was a large room with a *tatami* floor. The girl opened the wardrobe to show the futon mattresses and downy comforters inside. She glanced shyly at Naomi before talking to Keiko-san. Keiko-san smiled and replied, then turned to Naomi. "She wants to know what you are doing here."

Naomi paused, then shrugged. "I – I live here, in Japan, I mean," she said to Keiko-san. She then turned to the girl. "*Hokkaido ni sundeimasu. Ima oshogatsu yasumi desu* – I live in Hokkaido. Right now, I'm on New Year's holiday."

It was clear the girl found this hard to believe, as if a Canadian girl couldn't possibly be living in Japan. "*Watashi no namae wa Nami desu,*" she said, wide-eyed.

Naomi giggled at the girl's surprised look, and replied, "*Watashi wa Naomi desu.*"

Everyone chuckled over the close resemblance of their names. The girl stood there, as if wanting to say more, and then took a breath.

"We will serve dinner at seven o'clock," she said in heavily accented English. Then, bowing to Keiko and Sara, she left.

Later, they heard a knock at their door. Naomi opened it and Nami entered, smiling, carrying a tray which she set on the *kotatsu* by the window. Naomi, Sara and Keiko sat down and began lifting the lids off the many small dishes and bowls before them. Several things looked, and smelled, unfamiliar to Naomi.

"At the New Year, we eat special foods," Keiko explained. She reached for a bowl of long thin brown noodles. "We call this *toshi-koshi soba*. It means "year crossing" noodles. They are made of buckwheat. We eat them so that we can have a long life, like the noodles."

Naomi laughed, "Long noodles – long life. I get it. I'll eat any kind of noodle, long and thin like *toshi-koshi soba*, or short and fat like a *dango jiru* noodle. I love spaghetti, too."

Keiko smiled as she pointed out three wooden boxes on the table. "These are three dishes we serve together at New Year's time: boiled beans, boiled fish, and pickles."

"Mmm." Naomi inhaled the different aromas. "Smells delicious." She thought back to the Ukrainian Christmas foods she had served at her party. *Customs and traditions make life interesting*, she thought.

Keiko lifted the lid on a small tureen. A quite different, sweet, aroma wafted over. "This is *shiruko*. It is like a sweet soup made with red beans. Another Japanese tradition."

Naomi reached to take a ladleful but Sara stopped her. "That's for dessert. Let's get through the rest first, Naomi."

They ate until they could eat no more. It was only eight o'clock and Naomi, her stomach full, was beginning to feel tired. Her mind wandered to the year before, when she spent New Year's Eve with Imee, Lois and some other girls at Lois's farm. They had watched a TV music special and eaten popcorn, painted their fingernails and toes, and exchanged New Year's resolutions. A smile spread across her face as she relived it in her mind, and then she sighed. *This is not going to be a very exciting New Year's Eve, I think.*

There was a knock at the door. Nami peeked her head inside the room and exchanged some words with Keiko. "Would you like to visit with Nami and play some New Year's games?" Keiko asked Naomi. "Nami has some friends over."

Naomi sat up eagerly, and smiled at Nami. "I'd love to," she replied.

Naomi followed the girl to the family quarters, where two other girls were waiting. One of them clapped her hands as she saw Naomi, and said, "Hello. I'm Shiho. This is Mieko." Spread across the floor in front of them were many small cards lined up in columns. Naomi recognized the game, called *karuta*. She'd played this game before at Kiyoka's house.

"*Konbanwa.* I'm Naomi," Naomi said, playfully mixing Japanese and English together, hoping to make the girls laugh. The girls giggled some more, and Naomi was pleased. The girls moved over to make room for her around the cards on the floor. She kneeled beside Shiho, and soon they all began to play. One girl read a poem as the others tried to find the card that matched it. Each poem began with a certain sound, and the cards were written in the easy-to-read *hiragana*. Nami, Shiho, and Mieko were impressed with how well Naomi could play the game. And Naomi, too, was excited, when she realized that she was winning just as many cards as the other girls. Mieko took over the job as reader and was in the middle of a sentence when the door burst open.

"Woah! Woah! Woah!"

The four girls looked up, surprise on their faces. Mieko's mouth hung open mid-sentence. Nami's face quickly crinkled up in a smile. Naomi, whose back was to the door, whirled around.

"Aaaaaah!" Naomi screamed. She was face to face with two monsters. The wildly hairy things, one red and one blue, had rushed in and were shouting and darting their hideous bodies around the room. The girls cowered on the floor, but already they were beginning to laugh, leaving Naomi to look from them to the masked intruders with shock and surprise. The blue monster held a wooden staff with paper slips attached to it. The red monster, Naomi guessed a female, hefted a wooden bucket and a kitchen knife. The two monsters called out and strutted and stuck their ghoulish faces towards the four girls.

"*Namahage,*" Mieko said, and giggled. She stuck her face towards the red monster and cried out, "Woooo!" The red monster stopped and pulled away, then looked over to her blue companion for reassurance. Nami put a hand on Naomi's arm. "Don't worry, please," she paused, then explained, "My brother and sister."

The two monsters stopped when she said this. Slowly, they took off their masks, revealing a teenage boy and girl who looked remarkably similar. They smiled, and bowed politely to Naomi. "Happy New Year," the older boy said in thickly accented English.

Nami's mother and father entered the room, followed by Sara and Keiko, who had been observing the scene from the hallway. Keiko bowed to the mother and father, the owners of the inn, and said in Japanese, "Thank you for showing my Canadian friends this unusual New Year's custom."

"*Iie* – It's nothing," said the father, in his deep voice. Then, with a wink and a smile, he added that it was a good way to ensure that all the children in Akita were good boys and girls.

Later, a taxi came to take them to the Shinto shrine in the centre of town. Although it was almost eleven o'clock, there were large crowds of people everywhere. The shrine was bedecked with paper lanterns and decorations, and a real carnival atmosphere filled the air. From somewhere not too far away, a bell began to ring out, very slowly. The sound was loud and deep.

"Ah – the bells. The Buddhist temple will ring the bell 108 times around midnight," Keiko explained. She closed her eyes to better enjoy the sound.

"Why 108 times?" asked Naomi, curious.

"Well," Keiko began. "In Japan, Buddhism says that we humans have 108 earthly passions. In Buddhism, we must try to overcome these passions. The bell is struck once for every earthly passion."

"At this rate, the bell will toll for ages," Sara remarked.

"Yes, it will take about an hour," Keiko replied.

They walked up to the shrine. The air was chilly, but the people were bundled up for the cold, obviously used to it. Looking around, Naomi thought she could be at any winter carnival in Manitoba. Everyone looks the same when they are bundled up in fluffy parkas, winter boots, scarves and mittens.

"Naomi-san. Naomi-san." Naomi thought she heard her name. She turned and saw Nami, Mieko, and Shiho come running over.

"*Jiu...kyu...hachi* – Ten...nine...eight –" The countdown had begun!

"*Nana...roku...go*- Seven...six...five –" more and more people stopped to join in. "*Yon...san...ni...ichi...zero!*"

"Happy New Year!" Naomi shouted.

"Happy New Year!" Naomi heard people shout in familiar English, as well as Japanese. She hugged her mother and Keiko. A family nearby caught her eye and she reached over to shake their hands, too. The father offered to take a picture of the three of them with Naomi's camera.

Mom looks happy, Naomi thought as she watched her mother, standing with Keiko. A feeling of contentment welled up in her. *Last year, at Lois's sleepover, I would never have guessed that I'd be spending New Year's Eve like this. But – right here, right now – this is where I want to be.* The thought came out of nowhere and presented itself to Naomi with such clarity that she was surprised.

"I had a strange dream," Naomi whispered to Keiko early the next morning. "I was in the sky. I think I was climbing a mountain."

Keiko, an early riser, had been sitting quietly by the window, sipping tea. She raised her eyebrows. "Perhaps you were climbing Mount Fuji. That's a very good dream to have for your *hatsu-yume,* Naomi-chan," she whispered.

"What's *hatsu-yume?*" asked Naomi, propping herself up on one elbow on her futon.

"It means your first dream of the year. It is very auspicious – very lucky – to dream about Mount Fuji on your *hatsu-yume.* But it's also lucky to dream about eagles, and eggplants, too."

"Eggplants?" Naomi asked incredulously, then grimaced as Sara rolled over noisily on the other side of the room. They looked at each other with relief as they saw she hadn't woken up.

"Fuji-san, eagles, and eggplants. If you dream about any of these during your first dream of the year, it is a good thing," Keiko said, then added, "Maybe you were flying because you were an eagle, a beautiful golden eagle." As Naomi pondered this, Keiko said, "In any case, I think you will have a lucky year, Naomi-chan."

Naomi thought about her dream some more, trying to replay it in her mind. The feeling of flight and strength returned to her. *Maybe I will climb Fuji-san, someday,* Naomi thought. *But there are no mountains in Manitoba. I'll probably get half-way and get too tired to go on.* She tried to shrug off this thought, and a new one came to her: *My New Year's resolution is to not be so negative anymore and not to give mom a hard time about being here. From now on, I'll try to be more positive.*

Naomi smiled inwardly. She snuggled down deep into her futon and looked over at her mother, who was still asleep. She thought she detected a satisfied smile on her mother's face, as if she'd just heard every word of Naomi's promise.

English Lessons

"Happy birthday to me..." Naomi hummed to herself as she lay awake in bed. She looked out the window – it was another clear winter morning. She could hear her mother and Keiko in the kitchen downstairs, preparing breakfast: the sound of rice being poured into the rice cooker and the lid being shut; someone was chopping something – maybe tofu or some greens for the miso soup? "Time to start the day," she said out loud – which she often did when she was in an especially good mood – and pulled back the covers of her futon. A blast of crisp Hokkaido winter air engulfed her body and sent her scrambling for her fluffy comforter. Naomi made a snap decision that she deserved a few extra minutes cocooned in the warmth of her futon.

She snuggled back down inside her futon contentedly. Today was going to be special, she could feel it. But not only because it was her birthday. Today, Naomi was going to make another visit to Miss Ichimiya's class at Pippu Elementary School.

She walked into the kitchen just as her mother was setting the table. "Good timing, birthday girl. I was just going to call you down for breakfast." Sara reached over and gave her daughter a big hug.

"Happy birthday, Naomi-chan," Keiko smiled, and hugged Naomi as well. "Your mother and I have decided to take you and your girlfriends out to a special type of Japanese restaurant for dinner," she said, motioning for Naomi to take her seat at the table.

"Really? What kind of place?" Naomi asked.

"It's a surprise, of course, Naomi," Sara replied, "But I guarantee you'll think it's cool. Something to write home about."

Naomi giggled excitedly as she brought her soup bowl to her lips, and then changed the subject. "You know, this morning I am going to see Miss Ichimiya's class again. I've invented a big board game about Canada. It's kind of like 'Pin the tail on the donkey.'"

The two women smiled knowingly at each other and Keiko replied, "Yes, I haven't forgotten, Naomi. In fact, Takenaka-sensei called yesterday to say that you are invited to have school lunch with the class again. He said something about no *konnyaku*. What's he talking about?"

Naomi smiled as she fished with her chopsticks for the remaining bits of boiled tofu in her soup. "No problem. I love *konnyaku*, now."

"Are you nervous about your lesson?" Keiko asked.

"No, not really. I mean, I'm a little nervous, but I practised my lesson and I know that the game should work really well. When I planned it, I just tried to imagine I was one of the kids in the class. I'll ask Miss Ichimiya to explain the game to them in Japanese, just to be sure they understand."

"That's a good idea," Keiko said, and nodded, "You have good instincts as a teacher, Naomi, just like your mother."

Sara looked down at her watch. "Well, I'd better get going. Have a happy day today, Naomi. Don't forget to do your home-schooling this afternoon. No holiday for you, even if it is your birthday." She smiled at her daughter, who had risen and was helping Keiko clear away the dishes from the table. "I'll be home before six. Midori, Kiyoka and Ai will be here at 5:30, right?"

"Yes, I called them last night to remind them," Naomi replied, "I didn't tell them it was my birthday, though."

Sara stopped and looked back at her daughter, puzzled, "But Naomi, isn't that something you may have told them a long time ago?"

"Yeah, but they've probably forgotten."

"True. You never know, though. Word gets around," and with that cryptic comment, Naomi's mother waved goodbye.

Naomi opened the door to the school, and put on the oversized guest slippers from the shelf in the foyer. Slippers sliding on the linoleum tile, she walked over to the staff room. It was empty, except for the school "tea lady," and the school nurse. The tea lady, a cheerful elderly woman named Mrs. So, spotted Naomi at the door and motioned for her to come in. In Japan, many elementary and junior-high schools had a woman on staff who served tea and did clerical duties, but also had the important role of on-site *obaasan*, or grandmother, to the students. Naomi thought that Mrs. So fit that description nicely; with her portly figure and open manner, she reminded her of her own grandmother.

"The principal is coming, Naomi," Mrs. So said, handing Naomi some hot tea and a biscuit wrapped in paper.

"*Domo arigato, So-san,*" Naomi replied.

Takenaka-sensei emerged from the door to his private office, beaming and energetic as always. "Naomi-chan, good morning. The children in Miss Ichimiya's class are excited that you are visiting them again. And you know, today is a very special day. Do you know what day it is today, Naomi-chan?"

Naomi looked up, surprised at the unexpected question. Did he know something about her birthday? Takenaka-sensei grinned when he saw the perplexed look on her face. "Today is *Setsubun no hi*." She relaxed as Mr. Takenaka continued with his explanation. "All over Japan, we celebrate this day as the last day of winter." As an afterthought, he added, "Although in Hokkaido, we know that winter will stay here after February 3. In English, we say "Bean-throwing Day.'"

"Bean-throwing?" Naomi asked, curious.

"You might think it's a funny custom, like Halloween, perhaps. Here in Japan, we have spirits, too. On Bean-throwing Day, everyone throws beans to drive away all the bad spirits, the imaginary *oni*." Mr. Takenaka raised both hands to his temples with the index fingers pointing forwards as he said this word.

"*Oni?*" Naomi repeated the word and got her pocket dictionary out of her rucksack. She guessed the spelling, and in less than a minute was reading the English translation: devil.

Mr. Takenaka looked over her shoulder at the word on the page. "Yes, devil. On Bean-throwing Day, people go to the temple to throw beans and drive away the evil devils. Families will stand at the entrance to their homes and throw beans out the front door at the *oni*." He leaned forward and whispered, "Usually, the father plays the part of the devil. We shout "Fortune in, devils out!'"

Miss Ichimiya came to the staff room and greeted Naomi warmly. Naomi explained the activity she had planned for the lesson as they walked back to the classroom. When she turned the corner, she saw some familiar faces lingering at the doorway of Miss Ichimiya's classroom and laughed as she heard the words "Naomi-sensei" and "Su-to-ro-be-ri bronde." She was eager to get started and have fun.

Naomi took the large map of Canada out of her rucksack, unfolded it, and stuck it to the blackboard with her magnets. Then she took out the stack of pictures she had drawn and coloured. She showed the first picture to the class. "These are the Rocky Mountains," she said.

"Rocky Mountains," the children chorused three times.

Then, Naomi drew a line of X's over the Alberta/BC border on the map and posted the picture on top of them. She pointed at the picture on the big map, and said simply, "The Rocky Mountains are here."

Next, she showed the children another picture and said, "This is a polar bear." Again, the children repeated the words three times. She marked an X north of Churchill, Manitoba and posted the picture of the polar bear over it. "The polar bear is here."

Naomi repeated the process with a picture of a cowboy placed over southern Alberta; a totem pole placed on the Queen Charlotte Islands; the CN Tower over Toronto; a maple tree at sap-running time over south-eastern Quebec; and even a codfish attached off the coast of St. John's, Newfoundland. The children were mesmerized. Then Naomi showed the class a picture of Anne of Green Gables. As she guessed, the children knew the girl. It was a very popular story in Japan and most of the children had seen the real live "Anne" at Canadian World.

"*Aka ge no Anne* – Red-haired Anne," the children chorused, using the Japanese version of her name.

"Yes. This is Anne. Anne of Green Gables," Naomi pointed to the green shutters surrounding Anne as she said the words "Green Gables." Then she put the picture of Anne over Prince Edward Island and said, "Anne of Green Gables is here."

Naomi showed the class one last picture. They laughed when they saw it. "*Kawaii* – Cute," some of the girls said as Naomi let them linger over the picture. Then Naomi said, "This is Billy."

The boy in the third row knew. "Is it Miss Naomi's dog?"

"Yes. Billy is my dog," Naomi answered. And then, out of nowhere, a wave of homesickness overcame her. She looked at the picture of Billy for several moments, speechless. *The feeling never goes away*, she thought. *You can forget about it for a while, but it never goes away.* With a determined effort, she snapped herself back to the present, smiled at the class, and placed the picture of Billy over Portage la Prairie. "Billy is here," Naomi said, swallowing the lump in her throat.

"Now, let's play a game. Are you ready?" Naomi asked the class.

"Yes! Ready!" they answered back.

Naomi went to the board and removed all the pictures she had put up. She placed them on the chalk ledge underneath the big map of Canada, and then asked, "Where is the polar bear?" One girl came forward and tentatively reached for the picture of the polar bear and the magnet. Then, standing on her tip-toes, she posted the polar bear over the X that Naomi had drawn north of Churchill, Manitoba.

"The polar bear is ...," Naomi said, to prompt the student.

"The polar bear is here," the little girl repeated, as she flipped up the picture and pointed to the map underneath.

Naomi laughed at the girl's cleverness. "Very good," she said as she clapped and gestured for the class to clap along with her.

"Where is the CN Tower?" Miss Ichimiya asked. She'd barely finished the question, but everyone had their hands up, hoping for a chance to play the game.

"Taro," Miss Ichimiya said. A tall boy came forward. He quickly reached for the picture of the CN Tower but then hesitated as he looked all over the map. He paused and then looked at Miss Ichimiya with a nervous smile. Miss Ichimiya smiled back at him and then looked out to the rest of the children. "Help Taro. Where is the CN Tower?" The girl with the fat braids, who sat next to the tall boy, raised her hand. With a nod from her teacher, she came up and pointed to the X that Naomi had marked over Toronto.

"The CN Tower is here," she said, and shot the tall boy a wicked grin. The girl returned to her seat as the boy posted the picture, blushing.

They continued to play the game until there was one picture left. A boy cried out, "Where is Bee-ree? My name is Hiroyuki!" Everyone turned to the boy in the third row, and laughed.

"Come on up, Hiroyuki." Naomi invited him to the front of the class with a sweep of her arm.

The boy raced forward and put the picture of Billy over the picture of the polar bear. "Bee-ree is here!" Hiroyuki said proudly. With a funny wiggle, he returned to his desk, calling, "Bee-ree Bee-ree Bee-ree." The class laughed. Naomi laughed, and lovingly placed the picture of Billy over Portage la Prairie on the map. She looked at the picture for a long time, momentarily forgetting about the noisy children.

When the laughing died down, Miss Ichimiya spoke to the class. The children grew quiet, but their eyes sparkled. Miss Ichimiya turned to Naomi, "Thank you for teaching us about Canada, Miss Naomi. We hope you will come and visit us again. Takenaka-sensei would like to see you in his office, now."

Naomi was disappointed. She thought she was going to stay with the children for school lunch again. *Why am I being asked to leave now? What did I do wrong?* she asked herself. She wanted to know, but thought it would be better to do what Miss Ichimiya had told her. Naomi waved to the class and tried to smile a cheery goodbye. But inside, she was confused and hurt – as well as homesick all over again.

"Goodbye," the children said. Some of them waved. But some didn't.

Naomi's Bean-throwing Birthday

Miss Ichimiya had gathered Naomi's things and put them in her rucksack. Naomi walked out the door and down the corridor. Her face felt hot. She felt like she had been kicked out of class. *What did I do wrong?* she asked herself again. She headed to the principal's office and knocked on the door. Takenaka-sensei opened the door, smiling as always. Naomi saw that Mrs. Takenaka was there, and Keiko, too! A large flat box was on the table in front of them.

"Hello, Naomi-chan," Mrs. Takenaka and Keiko said.

"Hello, Takenaka-san. Keiko-san, what are you doing here?" Naomi replied with surprise as she took a seat next to the two women.

"Today is a special day, isn't it?" Mrs. Takenaka said, smiling.

"Yes, Takenaka-sensei told me. It's Bean-throwing Day," Naomi replied.

Mrs. Takenaka put her hand to her mouth, looked over at Keiko and then up at her husband. She laughed daintily. "Yes, it is. I almost forgot about that." She picked up the big box and passed it to Naomi with both hands. "*Tanjobi omedetto*, Naomi-chan. Happy birthday." Naomi stared at Mrs. Takenaka and Keiko, and then over at Takenaka-sensei, who had a big grin on his face. Slowly, with a bow, she took the box from Mrs. Takenaka.

"Happy birthday, Naomi-chan," Keiko said.

"Open it," Takenaka-sensei urged. As Naomi began to remove the wrapping, Mrs. So and the school nurse came into the room. Naomi removed the lid off the box, peeled away several layers of white tissue paper, and gasped in surprise. She was looking at a painting of pink cherry blossoms, white long-limbed cranes, and a golden sun – all on the richest royal blue background. But it wasn't a painting at all. Naomi touched the textured material with her fingertips. It was a Japanese kimono.

"Help her put it on, it will be lunchtime, soon," Takenaka-sensei said to the three women in Japanese. He turned to Naomi. "This is a gift from all of us. We thank you for teaching us about Canada," he said, then left the room.

Naomi couldn't believe it. What a surprise this day was turning into! Without protest, she let the four woman get to work. From the box, they removed not only the gorgeous kimono but the wide belt, the *obi*, and a large bow. There was a white cotton slip, a pair of pink sandals, and a pair of white socks, called *tabi*. Suddenly, Naomi felt ashamed for the doubts she'd had earlier. She was speechless with surprise and delight.

"It takes us more than an hour to dress ourselves properly in kimono," Mrs. Takenaka explained to Naomi. "But there isn't much time today, so why don't you just take off your sweater and we will put the kimono on over the rest of your clothes. If you like, someday, I can teach you how to dress up with the under-robes and everything. Okay, Naomi?"

Naomi nodded. Suddenly, she felt her woolly sweater being pulled over her head. Her arms were guided into long, roomy sleeves. The front of the kimono was tugged tightly across her chest and fastened with a ribbon. Naomi was turned around once, twice, as the school nurse wrapped the long *obi* tightly around Naomi's stomach, pulling brusquely. She struggled to remain on her feet. The women laughed and chattered to each other happily. Naomi giggled, too. Mrs. So reached to remove Naomi's socks and put on the white *tabi*. The socks, like a glove for her feet with the big toe separated from the other toes, fit perfectly. Naomi looked down as Mrs. So slipped the shiny pink sandals onto her feet. Keiko inserted the big wire hook of the ready-made bow into the back of the wide belt. They were finished. The women stood back and admired their work as Naomi pirouetted for them. There was a knock at the door.

"It's okay," said Keiko. Takenaka-sensei peeked in. "Lovely," he said approvingly as he looked at Naomi in her new kimono.

Then Takenaka-sensei said, "It's lunchtime now. You can go back to Miss Ichimiya's classroom, Naomi. They are waiting for you."

The bell had rung and Naomi hadn't even noticed! She went into the empty corridor and made her way up the stairs. *The children are probably already eating their lunch by now*, she thought as she made her way as fast as she could to Miss Ichimiya's classroom. She noticed how the narrow kimono made it necessary to take baby steps as she walked along the corridor. But at least the slippers were not going to fall off her feet! Naomi arrived at the classroom. Miss Ichimiya and her students were waiting. They all looked over and gazed in wonder.

"Waaaaa!"

"*Kirei* – Pretty," the children exclaimed.

Naomi looked at the board. The words "Happy birthday Miss Naomi" had been written in coloured chalk. Miss Ichimiya motioned for her to take the empty seat next to Hiroyuki.

"Happy basu-day too yoo, happy basu-day too yoo," the class sang out. "Happy basu-day, Miss Now-mee. Happy basu-day too yoooo." The children finished on a wobbly note and then dug into their school lunch with gusto. Naomi laughed and picked up her spoon.

"*Nan sai desuka* – How old are you?" a girl next to Naomi asked.

"*Jiu-san sai*," Naomi answered.

"Sirteen," another child said proudly, and then proceeded to amuse his group by ceremoniously spooning an oversized lump of rice into his mouth.

As the children finished cleaning up the lunch dishes and returning their desks into rows, Miss Ichimiya told Naomi that they would perform the bean-throwing custom on the front steps of the school. She led Naomi and her class to the front entrance, where they were joined by other children. Takenaka-sensei and his wife, Mrs. So and the school nurse were waiting for them. Mrs. So walked among the group, passing out handfuls of dried beans. Naomi stood at the top step next to Takenaka-sensei and the children. "We throw the beans and tell the *oni* to go away," he explained. He threw his handful to the side, scattering beans onto the snow next to the front steps.

Naomi felt someone pushing from behind. Out came Hiroyuki,

dancing around in front of the group wearing a strange little devil mask, with his hands at his temples and his fingers pointing forwards, just as Takenaka-sensei had done to mime the word *oni* – devil. Everyone burst out laughing. Naomi and the children threw their handfuls of beans out onto the snow. "Devils out! Fortune in!" Takenaka-sensei and the children said loudly in Japanese at Hiroyuki.

"Oni wa soto! Fuku wa uchi!" Naomi repeated, laughing.

Hiroyuki stopped and removed his mask. "Happy basu-day," he said, grinning at Naomi. Then, glancing at a smiling Takenaka-sensei, the boy assumed his *oni* role, pretended to be afraid and ran away into the crowd.

A plate of three tuna sushi rolls floated by on a boat in front of Naomi, as she thought about her day at school.

"Naomi! Aren't the tuna sushi rolls your favourite?" Kiyoka cried out beside her.

"Oops!" Naomi exclaimed and reached for the plate just before it sailed away out of reach. The little boat, now empty, sailed off in front of Ai, who was seated on Naomi's left.

They were all sitting at the bar of a very special sushi restaurant. At this place, various plates of sushi were placed on small wooden boats which were then sent around the circular bar in a kind of watery conveyor belt. If you wanted a certain kind of sushi, you simply waited for it to float by. When you were finished eating, the waiter would count the plates to tally the cost.

After everyone had eaten their fill of sushi, the girls each ordered some cake for dessert. When the cakes arrived, Naomi's mother ceremoniously placed one small candle in Naomi's piece of strawberry cheesecake, and the group sang the birthday song to her in Japanese. "Make a wish," Sara said.

As her friends crowded around, Naomi said, "This is the best birthday I ever had." Then, with her eyes shut tight, she made a wish for many more, and blew out the candle.

二十四

twenty-four

Girls' Festival

Naomi looked over at her calendar. "*Hina matsuri*," she said, reading the Japanese words. She could read more than four hundred *kanji* now, and was pleased with her progess. She quickly got dressed and headed to the kitchen. She spotted Keiko and Sara huddled over the kitchen table. They turned to look at her. The look on their faces told Naomi that something was up.

"What is it?" Naomi asked, "What are you looking at?"

Keiko smiled her serene smile and looked at Sara, who said, "Well, it looks like Midori can paint in at least half of the eye on that Daruma doll you told us about."

Naomi dashed over to the table to see the newspaper. As she scanned the text, something familiar jumped off the page and gave her a start: This week's *haiku* winner: Midori Takenaka, Pippu-cho, Hokkaido. Naomi's heart leapt. *Midori won!* She was thrilled for her friend. Then a second thought struck her – such good luck would not be striking twice. Naomi knew she wasn't going to win. She had submitted several of her best efforts, but lately had put the contest out of her mind. Naomi read Midori's winning poem with excitement:

> *stars shining bright*
> *on a silver platter moon*
> *night sky in winter*

"I'm going to call Midori," Naomi said, and ran to the phone.

"*Moshi-moshi*," Naomi heard Takenaka-sensei.

"Takenaka-sensei, it's me, Naomi!"

There was a laugh at the other end of the line. "Of course, Naomi-chan. Good morning. Did you read the English newspaper today?" he asked. Naomi heard a muffled noise, and then Midori's excited voice.

"I think my father is more excited about it than me," Midori said happily. Naomi laughed, picturing Takenaka-sensei's excitement.

"Congratulations, Midori."

"Thanks, Naomi. Now it's your turn. Then we can paint in the eye of the Daruma doll."

Naomi laughed and replied, "I'll do my best."

Midori laughed, too. "Today is *Hina matsuri*, Naomi-chan. Hinamatsuri means 'Girls' festival.' Today is a festival especially for all the girls in Japan."

"That's so cool," Naomi said, impressed. "Japan has a lot of neat festivals. Canada should have a girls' festival, too," she added with conviction as she looked over at her mother and Keiko.

"Well, why don't you start one when you get back to Canada, then, Naomi?" Midori asked. "Come to my house today, and I'll show you something. All Japanese families with girls in them have something special in their homes today."

"What is it?" Naomi's interest was piqued.

"That will spoil the surprise, Naomi. Come over after school and you will see."

"Okay, then, I'll see you at four o'clock. Bye, Midori."

As Naomi hung up the phone, Sara rose from the breakfast table and reached for the winter coat hanging over the back of her chair. "How are things going with your home-schooling, Naomi – are you keeping up?"

Naomi sat back in her chair and looked up at her mom. "I'm on schedule with the math and the science. English is no problem. And I'm working ahead on my independent project for social studies – it's all about Japanese festivals."

Sara and Keiko looked at each other and smiled. "Well then, you'll have a few more pages to add to it after today. Make sure you take your camera to Midori's house," Sara said as she reached over and kissed Naomi on the forehead.

"Now you've really got me wondering," Naomi said as she watched her mother head out the door. Cold air drifted back into the kitchen area as the door shut behind Sara.

Naomi and Keiko began to clear the breakfast table. As Naomi began to wash all the small dishes and cups, her mind drifted. She looked out the kitchen window at the grey winter morning and felt contented. *I'm happy – in spite of the cold grey morning. Actually, this kind of weather is no different from Manitoba. I'm happy, even though I go to school only part-time and spend the other part doing home-schooling by myself.* At this thought, Naomi chuckled. *Who would have thought that this is how I'd be spending grade eight?* She felt a flush of pride. *Things are working out, here.*

"A penny for your thoughts, Naomi-chan," Keiko's voice cut in and Naomi looked up from the kitchen sink.

"Thanks. I was just thinking about how I like my Japanese life." After a pause, she added, "And I remember how I complained to mom about being here, at first. I thought it was stupid. I wanted to go home so much."

Keiko put away some dishes and turned to face Naomi. "I'm glad to hear you say that, Naomi – your mom is, too. We are so proud of you for giving things a try. It was a big change, and big changes are never easy." Keiko moved closer and put her hand softly on Naomi's shoulder. "I'm glad you came to Pippu-cho, Naomi. It's been a big change for all of us. As for me, it's been a change for the better. Right from the start."

Naomi let the dish she was holding fall gently back into the water. She turned to hug Keiko and then drew back immediately – her wet hands were dripping on Keiko's dress. "Oh, I'm sorry," she said, as she reached for a dish towel.

Keiko laughed and hugged Naomi back to her. "That's okay."

Naomi buried her head on Keiko's small shoulder. Keiko was small – not much taller than Naomi, herself. But when Naomi hugged Keiko, it reminded her of Baba. All of a sudden, she missed Manitoba so much, and she began to cry. "I miss Baba – " Naomi croaked.

"You can cry, Naomi-chan. I know you miss them," Keiko said. They held each other close for several moments.

Naomi looked up into Keiko's eyes. "You are my Japanese grandmother," she said simply.

Keiko's eyes shone. "I'd like that very much, Naomi-chan. I can be your Japanese 'Baba,' if you like. You can call me *Obaachan*." She giggled. "Or maybe you should call me 'Obabachan.'"

Naomi choked on a laugh. Keiko rarely made a joke. "Will you be my Japanese Baba?" she asked.

Keiko laughed. "Of course," she replied.

Then she rested both her hands on Naomi's shoulders. "Naomi – you came here because your mother found a job here. And I know that you didn't want to be here. But you took the situation you found yourself in and you turned it around. You made it ... yours."

Keiko tried to find the words to explain what she wanted to say. "When you're young, you may not always have a say in the way things go in your life, and you might think it's not fair." She paused, reflectively. "But even when you're grown up, you can find yourself in a situation you may not like. So it's good to know how to change things around, even if it means changing only how you *think* about things, so you can be happy. I just want you to know that you have a lot to be proud of, Naomi-chan. Of course you are missing your home – but Japan is also your home, now."

Naomi looked up at Keiko. It was true. There was an ache in her heart for Canada. But she knew that Japan was a part of her life, now. *I'm learning to live with a lot of things here*, Naomi thought. She tried to think of what exactly she felt she had overcome – not just the school things, like learning to speak Japanese, or making new friends, or even getting used to the food. It was a lot more than that.

"When I first came to Japan, I have to admit my feelings were pretty negative. But now, I look back, and all the things I was afraid of are not a problem anymore," Naomi said to Keiko. But there was more. In a flash, she realized that many of these feelings were about herself, and not about other people or things. She felt an inner strength, a confidence in herself. She said simply, "I love this place, Keiko-san. I love Japan." Naomi threw her arms around the older woman. "I love you, Keiko-san – *Obaachan*."

Keiko stroked the young girl's hair. She looked out the window over the barren rice field, now covered in a thin layer of snow. She wiped away a tear that had fallen onto Naomi's red-blonde hair. "I love you too, my granddaughter."

Naomi felt energized for the rest of the day, working hard on her project about Japanese festivals. She had written several paragraphs to accompany the photographs that she had taken during her visit to the Sapporo Snow Festival, as well as the photos from New Year's Eve in Akita, and the Sports Day at Pippu Junior-High School back in November. Naomi flipped through her other photo albums: there was Ai and Makoto during *shichi-go-san* day, the neighbours dancing in a circle during the Obon Festival the week she arrived. Naomi stared for a long time at a picture that Keiko had taken of her on her birthday, standing beside Takenaka-sensei and his wife, wearing her new kimono.

So many memories, she thought. She glanced up at the calendar on the wall, and then over at the clock. It was time to meet Midori. Naomi grabbed her camera and said goodbye to Keiko before heading over to Midori's house. Midori was already at home by the time she arrived, and the small girl almost pulled Naomi through the door as she opened it.

"Come see my dolls for *Hina matsuri!*" she exclaimed, not waiting for Naomi to put on some house slippers, before skipping away into the living room. A few moments later, Naomi entered the room, and saw Midori proudly standing next to the most extraordinary doll collection she had ever seen. Naomi counted eighteen dolls of various sizes and shapes placed on a tiered platform that rose to a height taller than Midori herself.

Midori pointed to the top tier, to two dolls, dressed ornately. "This is the Heian Imperial Court. It's a long time ago. These are my Emperor and Empress." Midori then pointed to the next tier, where three lovely female dolls stood in their elegant costumes. "They are ladies-in-waiting," Midori explained, then added, "I looked that word up in the dictionary." She continued, pointing below to the five male dolls on the tier below, "They are court musicians." On the tier below were six smaller dolls that Midori called ministers, along with plates of oranges and rice cakes. Finally, on the bottom tier, stood three guards between a small orange tree and a small peach tree.

"Midori, it's beautiful," Naomi said in awe, as she reached forward and gingerly lifted one of the ladies-in-waiting off the shelf. It was gorgeous, and obviously very old. She carefully put it back in its place.

"Every home will have this doll collection – if there are little girls in the house. We put it up for Girls' Festival. Some are much smaller, maybe only the two dolls at the top, the Emperor and Empress. But some are bigger, too," Midori explained. "This collection is from my grandmother. Now, it is my mother's. Someday, it will belong to me," she said proudly.

Naomi looked at the pride on her friend's face. *Every home with a girl in it must have one of these doll collections*, Naomi thought. Her eyes lit up with a special idea.

Back at home, later that evening, Naomi went to Keiko and held out a small box.

"What's this, Naomi?" Keiko asked.

"Oh, just a little present for my Japanese grandmother," Naomi replied, her eyes twinkling.

Keiko carefully lifted the lid off the little box. Inside was a miniature pair of dolls, made from Japanese origami paper, with a small gold screen behind them. The entire doll set was no larger than Naomi's hand.

"Midori said that, during Girls' Festival, every house with a girl in it should have a doll set like this," Naomi said happily, then looked over mischievously at her mother. "And, I thought: Well, *I'm* here. So I thought you should have one in your house."

Keiko looked over at Naomi and then at Sara. Her eyes sparkled as she held up the small pair of dolls. After several moments, she spoke. "Thank you, Naomi-chan. It is the loveliest gift."

二十五

twenty-five

Back to School

Naomi and her mother were looking hard at the mirror, studying Naomi's reflection. The two-week break between grades was over. It was the beginning of April, and today Naomi was starting grade eight at Pippu Junior-High School.

"Naomi, your skirt looks like it could be taken down a little – have you grown that much in just a few months?" Sara asked as she surveyed her daughter in her school uniform.

Naomi peered into the mirror and then looked down at her navy pleated skirt. "Hmm, I think you're right. They're pretty strict about hemlines at school." She looked at her mother, rolled her eyes, and grinned.

Sara laughed. "It's different, isn't it, being a student in Japan. I remember when I was teaching in Kyushu. Very different," she finished, thoughtfully.

"Yes. Not better, or worse, I suppose. Just different," Naomi said. "But sometimes, the differentness is pretty wonderful," she said, adding, "There are a lot of things the same, too. Good friends, good food – "

Sara's face lit up. "Naomi, I'm so glad you are coming to love Japan like I do. And I know it's not easy, sometimes. Are you nervous about going back to school?"

Naomi nodded matter-of-factly, "Yes. I'm not sure that all my friends will be in the same class as me this time. It would be nice if Midori, Kiyoka, Ai, and Kenji were all in the same class."

Sara grinned mischievously. "Kenji?"

Naomi blushed, embarrassed. "Mom, he's my friend. He likes to talk to me in English, but sometimes I think he's just teasing me."

"Maybe he likes you, Naomi," Sara said, still smiling.

Naomi turned to face her mother head-on. "Not you too, mom!" she groaned good-naturedly, then became serious. "Actually, when I first went to Pippu Junior-High School, Kenji teased me a lot. It made me not want to even go, sometimes. But then, after a while, I realized that he was – kind of – a leader in class, so I think he felt he had to say something to me. I think he's actually kind of shy."

"I can understand that, Naomi. After all, how many Canadian girls does he know?" Sara asked.

I wonder if the two mean-looking girls will be in my class, Naomi thought. Their attitude towards her hadn't changed at all over the last few months. She saw the secret hostile stares almost every time she sat in class. Naomi had never said a word about them to anyone, although she felt that Midori suspected something. *It doesn't matter – I just have to ignore them. They are not important in my life*, Naomi told herself forcefully. She realized that she could think about this secret problem and not get as worried about it as she used to.

"You'd better get moving, Naomi. When do the opening day ceremonies begin?"

Naomi checked the clock by her bed. It said 7:45. "Yipes – you're right. I told Midori I'd be by her place at ten to eight. The ceremony starts at 8:30."

With a quick kiss on the cheek for her mother and Keiko, Naomi grabbed her school bag and set off down the sidewalk. "Please let some of my friends be in my homeroom this year. I don't want to be alone," Naomi whispered to herself as she neared Midori's home. *What if no one is?* She began to feel the knot in her stomach again. She was surprised, it had been so long since she felt that awful, dread feeling. Some boys from another grade ran past and laughed in her direction. Naomi sighed. *Challenges every day. Sometimes it doesn't seem to get any better.* She looked up and saw other familiar students walking to school. They were waving to her. She smiled and waved back, encouraged by their friendliness. "And, then again, some things do get better," she whispered. She smiled a smile of relief and shut her eyes to face the northern spring sun.

"Good morning!" Naomi heard, and opened her eyes. Midori was standing at the end of her drive. The two girls quickly fell in step for the short walk to school.

"You will like the opening ceremony today, Naomi. It is a very special day for the new children who are starting the first grade of junior-high school," Midori explained, "I remember when I was starting first grade last year. I was so scared and nervous. I was afraid the older children wouldn't like me, or they would tease me because I was new and didn't know anything. But now it is my job to help the new students, because I am in second grade, now."

"In Canada, I would call myself a grade eight student. Here in Japan, I am a grade two student again," Naomi said, and laughed. Midori laughed, too. "What about the students in grade nine – or rather, grade three?" asked Naomi.

"They are too busy preparing for high school," Midori replied. "In Japan, the second grade students must help the younger students settle in. You will see."

Naomi and Midori entered the school yard, which was buzzing with excitement. It was easy to see which children were new. Naomi felt a little sorry for them, as they warily eyed the older, more self-assured students. *I was like them, once*, Naomi reminded herself. Then the idea came into her mind: *But now, I can look back and say that everything turned out okay in the end.* She caught the eyes of three little grade one girls, who were huddled together, looking at her with wide-eyed wonder. She giggled and waved at them. The three girls almost jumped in surprise.

Naomi and Midori caught up with Ai and Kiyoka and went to find their new homerooms for the year. Each room had a list of students posted outside the door. Ai looked over at Midori and Naomi with a sad look before walking off slowly to another classroom down the hall. Naomi was disappointed. Not even the discovery of being in the same class with Midori, Kiyoka and even Kenji, could make her feel better. She would miss Ai's antics. Having Ai in class always made things interesting.

Naomi's new homeroom teacher came in and asked everyone to find their seats, explaining that they would go into the auditorium for the opening ceremonies in a few minutes. Naomi found that she was seated right behind Kiyoka this year. Kiyoka turned around in her chair and beamed as Naomi took her seat. Naomi looked around the room to find Midori in an opposite corner. She spotted Kenji, who was looking right at her with a big grin and a wave. She felt her face grow hot as she quickly faced the front of the class.

Within moments, the bell rang and all the grade two and three classes began filling the school auditorium. Naomi was surprised to see rows of parents and a head table of town dignitaries already seated in the auditorium. The grade two and three students filed into rows of chairs at the back of the gym, leaving several long rows of chairs empty at the front. Then, an expectant hush filled the cavernous hall. The principal walked solemnly to the stage and made a short speech at the podium. Naomi tried hard to understand what he was saying, but could only understand the gist; about welcoming the new students to their new lives as junior-high-school students. The crowd burst into applause and Naomi could see two columns of students excitedly and self-consciously walking down the aisle to take their seats at the front of the gym. She stared at their nervous and excited faces. Then the teachers were introduced to the new students. After a few more speeches of encouragement from the mayor of Pippu-cho and the head of the parent-teacher association, the entire group rose to sing the national anthem and the school song. Naomi felt proud to be singing in Japanese alongside her schoolmates. *If my friends in Portage la Prairie could see me now*, she thought.

Later, after the day's classes, Naomi and Kiyoka went to Kendo Club. They knew that today, many of the new students would be coming to observe and decide whether they wanted to join. For that reason, special demonstrations and matches were going to be played. Naomi had been looking forward to this day for some time. She had worked hard on her kendo technique since she joined back in December, and she knew she had improved greatly since that match in gym class on her first day of school. She could still remember lying sprawled on the gym floor, looking up at the face of her opponent that day – Darth Vader, with her sniggering sidekick.

They had kept their distance these past few months, although Naomi could always count on the same old silent sneers whever the girls managed to catch her eye. After a while it had simply become a bore – an annoyance, nothing more.

So it was a shock when Naomi and Kiyoka eagerly bounded into the gym and found the two mean-looking girls there ahead of them.

Naomi's old nemesis smiled sweetly at them both as they came close.

"We're joining the Kendo Club this year," the taller girl said in Japanese. The two girls grinned at each other and reached for some kendo equipment. Trouble was brewing.

The room soon filled with club members and prospective members from all three grades. Mrs. Wada welcomed all the new students and gave a brief explanation of the equipment. The club members lined up in pairs and demonstrated the various moves. Naomi found herself relaxing during the drills as she concentrated on her technique. She was impressed with Kiyoka's improving skills as well, and smiled proudly behind her mask.

The club members played several good, entertaining rounds for the group, and then Mrs. Wada asked for a volunteer from the new students. In a flash, Darth Vader had raised her hand. Just as quickly, Naomi stepped forward.

"I'll play a match with her," she said in Japanese. She didn't notice the look on the mean-looking girls' faces as she put on her mask and strode confidently into the centre of the ring of students. Naomi bowed solemnly to her opponent and prepared to begin the match. She took several deep breaths. She cleared her mind of distractions, focusing only on her body and the bamboo sword in her hands, and how they would soon be working together. When Mrs. Wada gave the signal, Naomi was ready, delivering the first well-placed strike to her opponent's wrist. Several more followed in quick succession to her opponent's torso. A point for Naomi.

The crowd broke into cheers and both girls stepped back, waiting to recommence the match. Darth Vader didn't stand a chance. At the next signal, Naomi lunged forward with the same decisive movements, and a definitive strike to her opponent's helmet. It was another obvious point. The match was over before it had begun, it seemed. Darth Vader hung her masked head. The room fell silent. Naomi couldn't remember a match being won so quickly.

It was a humiliating way to be defeated, Naomi had to admit, and she felt sorry for the girl standing across from her. Instinctively, she removed her helmet and mask and moved towards her opponent. She put out her hand in a western-style handshake. "Good match," she said, and smiled.

The girl behind the mask said nothing, but reached tentatively for Naomi's outstretched hand and held it for several seconds. Then she turned on her heel and walked slowly into the changing room with her only friend not far behind.

The crowd broke up as Mrs. Wada announced the end of the session. Naomi found herself staring at the changing room door as Kiyoka came up to congratulate her. *It's not about winning*, was all Naomi could think. She wanted to tell them that. No matter what happened between herself and those two girls from now on, Naomi felt strong enough to forgive them.

twenty-six

Golden Week

The cold and grey drizzly day marked the start of Golden Week, a holiday time at the beginning of May when families often go away on short vacations. Naomi and her mother had decided to stay closer to home and take a short, four-day excursion by train straight to the northern coast of Hokkaido.

"Mom, why can't we ride the trains in Canada the way we do here in Japan?" Naomi asked, her eyes still glued to the countryside rolling by. "I love trains – there's so much to see."

"Well, Naomi, for one thing, the distances between places are a lot greater in Canada. That's why people prefer to fly," her mother replied. "And there isn't this much to see when you're on the train through the Canadian prairies, let me tell you. I remember I took the train from Winnipeg to Vancouver when I was your age. It was sooo long and boring, until you got to the Rockies. Then I wanted to sleep with the window blinds up so I could see outside while I lay in bed."

"I know what you mean," Naomi replied, and gazed out the window again. Her attention was caught by some strange flags flying in the sky. They were round, like a kind of windsock or strange kite, and attached to long bamboo poles standing next to people's homes. "Do you know what those are, mom?"

"Those are flying carp. People fly them to show that they have children. It used to mean that there were boys living in the house –

they would put up one for each boy in the family. But now it doesn't matter if it's a boy or a girl. They are put up at this time of the year. Today is May 5th – *Kodomo no hi*," Sara answered.

"Children's Day! That's another custom that we should start back in Manitoba," Naomi laughed.

"Every day is Children's Day," Sara said, and Naomi grimaced good-naturedly. How often had she heard that! Naomi enjoyed spotting the different flying carp as the train rolled by each little village and town. After a while, she settled back in her seat and turned her attention to the book in her lap, *Totto-chan: The Little Girl at the Window.*

Sara put her own book down, and smiled when she saw what Naomi was reading. "I remember reading that book. Totto-chan has a lot of inner strength, for such a young girl." She looked for a few moments at the cover of the book, then returned to her own novel.

Naomi looked at the picture of Totto-chan on the cover and then at the cold landscape on the other side of the thin pane of glass that was the train window. *What is inner strength?* she asked herself. *Do I have it?*

More flying carp came into view as the train approached another small town. Naomi put her book aside, and pulled her notebook out of her duffel bag. She began to write:

> *rippling in the wind*
> *fish are flying in the sky*
> *kodomo no hi*

"Three hours until we get to Wakkanai," Sara said.

"What do you mean: you don't know?" asked Naomi.

Naomi's mother paused, confused, and then laughed, "I didn't say *wakaranai*. I said: Wakkanai. That's the town at the northern tip of Japan.

Naomi giggled back, "I knew that. I was making a joke."

"My, you're getting so good at your Japanese, you can even make a pun." Sara reached over and gave her daughter a kiss. "You've got me beat."

Naomi and her mother spent a day and a night in Wakkanai, Japan's northernmost town, and then travelled east across Hokkaido to Rausu, a small town on the seacoast of Shiretoko Peninsula. Rausu was famous for its hot springs and its wildlife. While taking a bus into Rausu, Naomi had spotted a bear and several deer, and had seen several white-tailed eagles flying overhead.

Naomi and her mother checked into a small traditional inn at the edge of Rausu and then headed to a hot spring not far from the ocean. From where they sat in the small hot spring pool, they could see a large island. It loomed up into one large mountain covered in trees. More eagles flew overhead. It was a remote and wild place.

"You see that island over there, Naomi?" Sara asked.

"Yes, I see it."

"That's not Japan," said Sara.

"What do you mean?" asked Naomi.

"Well, it used to belong to Japan, but it doesn't now."

Naomi was intrigued. "Well, what country is that, then – Korea?"

"It's Russia."

Russia! The word went through Naomi like a jolt. So many people back in Manitoba had come from Russia and its neighbour, Ukraine. But she was far from Ukraine, Naomi knew. Russia was bigger than she had ever imagined. She looked across the frozen water at the tiny island. It was so close! "Russia! You can see it from here!" Naomi cried out, thrilled. "I can see Russia?"

"Yes, that's Kunashiri Island," Sara began. She dried her hands on a nearby towel and gingerly grabbed her travel guidebook. She flipped to a map of northern Japan and showed it to Naomi. "There are other islands; Etorofu, Shikotan and the Habomai Islands, that Russia took over from Japan at the very end of World War Two. Of course, the Japanese were not very happy about it – especially those that were living there."

Naomi looked at the map with interest, then at her mother, "Who lives there now?"

"The population is almost all Russian, now, Naomi. But there are many Japanese who live here that would like to go to those islands to visit their ancestors' graves," Sara explained, then continued. "Russia calls them the Kuril Islands. Actually, for the last few years, the Russian people who live there, and the Japanese here, have been making exchange visits – no visas or passports needed. But it's still a diplomatic problem between the two countries."

Naomi was intrigued, her thoughts focused on the unusual fate of the islands, once a part of Japan and now a part of Russia. She gazed at the big mountain in front of her and then again at the map. On paper, the islands looked like nothing more than tiny strips in the sea.

Sara smiled. "It's a big old wide world out there, isn't it, Naomi?" she commented.

"It sure is, mom," Naomi replied, her eyes shining.

Sara observed her daughter's happy face for a long time before she spoke. She hesitated, and said, "Naomi ... I have to tell you ... I mean, we always knew – "

Naomi looked at her mother, who now seemed to be at a loss for words. "What is it, Mom? Just say it. It can't be all that bad."

Sara smiled. "Of course, Naomi. We always knew this was the plan. But before we left Pippu-cho the other day, I got a phone call. I received confirmation about a teaching job in Winnipeg. I need to be there at the beginning of August, Naomi. And we need to find a place to live and get settled in." She paused. "That means we'll be leaving Japan a little earlier than we planned."

Naomi looked at her mother. "How early?" she asked cautiously.

"Well, I think we should leave in the middle of July. Maybe sooner."

Naomi looked down. Her mind felt oddly numb. *I always knew this was the plan, that we would go home after a year. And I've always wanted to go home,* she thought. *So why do I feel so rotten?* She realized that the idea of leaving two weeks early wasn't the problem – it was the idea of leaving Japan altogether. Naomi took a deep breath. "I want to go home," she said to her mother. Then she lowered her eyes. "But I don't want to leave Japan."

Naomi felt her mother's arm slip across her shoulders. "Naomi, everything will be okay," she said quietly.

A moment of panic swept over Naomi. *What if I leave here and never come back?* her thoughts raced. *What if I leave here and never see Keiko-san again – or Midori, or Ai, or Kiyoka? Everyone at Pippu Elementary School?* Her eyes began to sting. She focused her eyes on the mountain across the strait; amazingly, a part of Russia.

"Naomi, are you okay?" Sara asked.

Naomi looked over at the mountain. She forced a smile. "I'm glad to go home, mom. After all, Japan, and everyone I know here, will always be a part of my life, right?"

Sara smiled, relief showing clearly in her eyes. "Japan will always be a part of your life, if you want it to be. It's up to you, Naomi. It's a matter of will."

Naomi looked at her mother. "What do you mean – will?"

"Your will – it's what you want and believe and intend. You are in charge, Naomi. If it is your will that Japan stays a part of your life, then it will be."

She swallowed hard. "I believe that, mom."

Sara hugged her. "That's my girl. Now – heading back to Canada leaves us with not much more than a couple of months. We owe a lot of people thanks. It's time to start planning our goodbyes, and our thank-yous.

Naomi nodded. "I'll miss Keiko-san, though. Can she come and visit us someday?" It sounded so futile, just a simple invitation. Keiko would probably never come.

Sara threw her head back and laughed, "Of course. Keiko-san can come visit us whenever she wants."

Naomi smiled, then asked hopefully, "Then, can Midori, Kiyoka and Ai come too?"

"Yes, they can come, too, Naomi. If they want to badly enough, they will. Who knows when?" Sara said.

"I can't wait to tell everyone about Japan and Pippu-cho back home," Naomi said. She dunked her head under the hot water. When she raised her head, it was enveloped in steam. The water was so relaxing. She sat back, rested her head against a rock and gazed up at the grey sky above her. Then she leaned over to face her mother. "Mom."

"Hmmm," replied her mother, eyes closed.

"Remember you said that if I wanted to talk about why you and dad got divorced ..."

Sara opened her eyes and focused them on Naomi.

"... you would talk to me about it."

"Yes, Naomi. I owe you that much. It's just that I don't know where to begin. I've asked myself so many questions about it, too, over the years," she said.

"All I know about your dad and I is that we were very young when we got married." She paused and smiled reflectively, "Going back to Kyushu for Christmas made me remember some things."

"What kinds of things?" Naomi asked.

"Well, the feelings I had, for one thing. I loved it there – it was an exciting time for me, being on my own for the first time. But there were other feelings, too." Her expression darkened.

"What other feelings?" Naomi asked, curious.

"Feelings of loneliness, I suppose," Sara replied. "Don't get me wrong, I loved my little village and all the people there. But your father was there for me in a way that no one else could be. We were in the same boat, in a way. Here in Japan, together, we had a lot in common. We were young and we relied on each other – too much, I suppose. But when we went back to Canada, the situation was different." Sara looked over at the sea and crouched deeper in the water to warm up. "We grew up, and we grew apart." She looked at her daughter. "I don't know if I can explain it any better than that, Naomi."

Naomi could see that her mother was explaining the situation honestly, searching for the right words. She knew that it wasn't an easy thing to talk about.

"Mom, whatever happened – I don't blame you for dad not being around," Naomi said slowly. "I know that it was as hard for you as it is for me. Maybe it is, still."

Sara looked at Naomi. "It is, honey," she replied softly. "It is, still."

Naomi hugged her knees and crouched down lower, until the hot water rose to a point just beneath her chin. She looked down her nose at the steaming water. "I guess we are all just doing the best we can. That's what you said when we first came to Japan. I know I was mad at you, back then. But I think I understand a little better about what you mean, now."

She counted the weeks until the middle of July. Only ten weeks to go! How could she say thank you and goodbye to everyone in Pippu-cho? *It's going to have to be something special, whatever I do*, she thought. Slowly, an idea began to form in Naomi's mind.

twenty-seven

Cherry Blossom Time

"I woke up one morning and what did I see? Pink popcorn is poppin' on the old cherry tree – or something like that. How does that old rhyme go, anyway? Look, Naomi! Do you see what I see?" Sara and Naomi were riding their bikes along the levy in Pippu-cho on the way to Asahikawa. It was a sunny and warm May morning, a perfect day for a picnic in the park with friends. Sara stopped her bike and Naomi pulled up behind her.

"What is it, mom?" asked Naomi.

Sara pointed at the rows of trees that lined the levy. The cherry blossoms were starting to bud, looking for all the world like little pale pink kernels of popcorn scattered among the branches.

"It's starting! Cherry blossom time is starting in Pippu-cho!" Sara said excitedly. Naomi looked over at her mother. Her eyes were bright. "I love the *sakura*. Just wait, Naomi. In a week or so, all the cherry trees in Pippu-cho will be covered in fluffy pink snow. To me, it really is the most beautiful sight in all Japan."

Naomi had heard a lot about the legendary cherry blossom time in Japan. Because it was warmer in the south, the cherry blossom season started there first, moving across the country from south to north. Since early April, Keiko, Naomi and her mother had followed its progress on the nightly news. Keeping track of the cherry blossom "front," as it was called in Japan, was important to everyone. The first sightings were in Kagoshima, Oita City, Kyoto, then Tokyo, Sendai, Morioka, then Sapporo. And now – Pippu-cho.

"Just you wait, Naomi-chan, just you wait," Sara laughed as she got back on her bike and rode away. Naomi was glad to see her mother so happy. *She's probably happy I'm not hassling her about being in Japan anymore. And happy that she's got a job in Winnipeg so she can take me back home.* As Naomi rode along the levy, she thought about all the times she had argued with her mom about coming to Japan. She couldn't imagine feeling that kind of anger, these days. She had a different problem, now. It was already May. They were going home in less than two months.

Her legs pumped to keep up to her mother, who looked back from time to time to stick out her tongue and laugh at her daughter. Despite the cool breeze, the spring sunshine was surprisingly warm. Naomi slowed down to undo the buttons of her coat. *I need more time,* she found herself thinking. *There's so many things I have to see here, so much to do. I can read five hundred kanji – I want to get to a thousand. I want to learn more karaoke songs with Ai, Kiyoka and Midori. I want to get better at kendo. I want to get a haiku poem published in the newspaper.* She smiled at this last thought, knowing that Takenaka-sensei would be especially impressed if she won. Naomi visualized herself painting in the second eye of the Daruma doll. She remembered the day that Midori had won the haiku contest. It was months ago, but she remembered Midori's happiness like it was just last week. "Time is going too fast," Naomi said out loud to the cherry trees as she cycled on by.

Her thoughts turned to her three best friends in Japan and she was surprised to feel hot tears prick her eyes. She thought of Ai – big, bold Ai, who wasn't afraid to speak, in any way she could, to make a point. The girl who could always make Naomi laugh. And there was lovely, graceful Kiyoka, the girl who told her a secret the day they first met. Naomi knew that, under Kiyoka's calmness and serenity, there was great strength and determination. And, of course, there was Midori. Little Midori. A green elf. The one who grabbed Kiyoka and tried to run when she saw Naomi looking at them through the front window on Halloween night. *Her English is amazing now,* Naomi thought with pride.

How can I ever say goodbye to them now? How can I thank them all for all their friendship? Naomi rode along in the sunshine, thinking. She thought about her special idea and said out loud, "It's going to be good – a big thank-you to everyone in Pippu-cho. And today, I'm going to start by doing something nice for my friends in the English Club."

Naomi and her mother rode down the levy towards the central park in Asahikawa. From a distance, Naomi could see a bunch of bicycles leaning up against the fence and some of the English Club members spreading blankets out under some cherry trees. She smiled; the English Club had grown since April, and now had fifteen members. A car pulled up nearby, and Ai and another English Club member came out, lugging a large box that looked like a stereo speaker.

"Ooooooeee, Naomi! Karaoke!" Ai cried out, and waved.

Naomi parked her bike and started helping set up the picnic with the others. Then, from her rucksack, she pulled out her surprise for the club: a large yellow envelope filled with other envelopes – letters from Canada! Naomi smiled with excitement as she passed out an envelope to each member of the group. She could tell that everyone was excited. They pulled out their letters and photos and all began to read.

Naomi bounced from one person to another, helping those having difficulty reading the English words.

"This is great!" Naomi heard a few people say.

"*Penfrendo!*" someone else exclaimed happily.

Naomi watched with a mixture of pride and relief as the group began reading their letters aloud, showing the pictures of their new penpals to each other. As soon as she'd returned from her Golden Week vacation, Naomi had asked Imee and Lois to find fifteen people at school who wanted to write to a Japanese penpal. Naomi recalled how they had e-mailed her, saying it had not been hard to find fifteen takers! Imee and Lois were among the group who had written letters introducing themselves, including photographs as well. Naomi looked around the group, eager to see which of her friends here would be writing to Imee and Lois. She was delighted to see that Kiyoka was busy studying the letter from Imee, and that Kenji was going to be Lois's penpal.

"Now you all have Canadian penpals, and you can practise your English with them, too," Naomi said. "Who knows? Maybe someday you will visit Canada – or they will come here – and you can meet them. It's up to you." Then, reaching into her rucksack again, she pulled out what looked like a handful of string.

"What's that?" Kenji asked.

Naomi knew how ceremony and ritual were an important part of Japanese life. She stood up and said solemnly. "I have lived in Pippu-cho for ten months now. And I have been a student at your school since November. I would like to thank you for being my friends. I have enjoyed being a member of the English Club with you." She cleared her throat and continued. "As special assistant to the Pippu Junior-High School English Club, I would like to present to all the members a special memento. I hope you will remember all the fun times we have had together." She took one of the strings. It was a friendship bracelet that she had made herself by knotting multicoloured strings together in intricate patterns. Imee had taught her how to make them last summer, before she had come to Japan.

Naomi called out the names of the English Club members one by one. Each boy and girl came forward and stood before her as she tied the friendship bracelets around their left wrists. They bowed together before the members took their seats on the blankets. Naomi continued the ceremony until everyone had a bracelet, and were admiring the lovely designs and colours.

"You made this?" Ai asked Naomi, as she held out her wrist for everyone to see. Naomi had given Ai a bracelet made of red and white threads, knotted together in a way that looked like a miniature Canadian flag.

"I did, " Naomi replied proudly. "And if you want, I'll teach you in our English Club next week."

It was late in the afternoon when the party ended. Everyone was enjoying themselves in the warm spring air, singing karaoke, eating, and talking about their new penpals. Kenji, who was acting as chair of this special meeting of the English Club, thanked Naomi for organizing such a wonderful idea. "Naomi makes English Club fun," he said, and everyone laughed, nodding their heads in agreement. Naomi smiled to herself. There was more to come.

二十八

twenty-eight

Learning to Climb

Keiko and Naomi were enjoying one of their usual weekly lessons together, over lunch at a restaurant in Asahikawa. If anyone had walked by the little cafe that noon hour, they would have noticed the serene Japanese woman smiling across the table at the young blonde girl, chattering away animatedly. Naomi had good reason to be excited; she and her mother were planning a trip. But it wasn't just any trip. Next week, they were going to climb the highest mountain in Japan, Mount Fuji.

Fuji-san, as the mountain is known to all Japanese, is not only the highest mountain in the country, but also the most revered. When Naomi first saw pictures of it in a school book years ago back in Canada, she thought it was the most beautiful, perfectly formed mountain she had ever seen. These feelings only became stronger when she saw it for herself at Christmas.

A long-dormant volcano, Fuji-san rose up with perfect symmetry. The uppermost third was covered with a layer of snow, and topped by an enormous crater. Naomi was excited, but deep down, she wondered if she really could pull it off. "Keiko-san, I can't believe that they'll let just anyone climb the highest mountain in the country. How difficult is it?" she asked.

Keiko thought for a moment and then looked at Naomi straight in the eye. "In Japan, we say that it is foolish NOT to climb Fuji-san once in our lives. And, I believe, during the course of a Japanese person's life, most of them try. But it is not an easy climb for ordinary people like us, Naomi. I still remember when I climbed it – how, as I climbed, I kept looking up to the top and the mountain just kept getting steeper and steeper. At one point, I thought I would never make it."

"How old were you when you climbed Fuji-san?" Naomi asked.

"I was about your mother's age. At that time, I was quite fit. But it was difficult. To me, it is still one of the most physically challenging things I have ever done."

"In the beginning, the climb is not so hard," she continued. "At its base, Fuji-san is very big and there are a few roads leading to different routes. A bus takes you about two-thirds of the way up, to station five. But even with the headstart, the climb is long. I think it took me about eight hours to go up and then come down. Actually, coming down is much faster. Part of the mountainside is like sand – black sand – and you can sort of 'shoosh' your way down. I think it took us only about two or three hours to get back down from the top.

"I remember, at one point, becoming very discouraged," Keiko said. "I could see that the most difficult part lay ahead of me, still. I looked across the pathway and saw a man with a young girl. He was obviously a grandfather with his granddaughter – he looked about sixty years old, and the little girl was younger than you. I was so surprised to see them there. He was pouring some drink for her from a thermos, and they both looked over at me and smiled."

She paused, and looked out the window of the coffee shop. Naomi waited. "At that moment, I knew I would make it to the top. It didn't matter if it was going to be difficult. I would just – as you say in English – take it one step at a time."

Keiko looked across at Naomi and said, "Climbing the highest mountain in Japan may seem like an impossible thing, but there is no reason why you can't succeed. And when you get there, you might look back and say, 'Maybe I can even do it again.'"

Naomi thought about what Keiko had just said. Then she had an idea. "Keiko-san, if that's how you feel, why don't you come with us?"

The woman threw her head up and laughed. "Well, Naomi, I told you what we say in Japan – that it is foolish not to climb Fuji-san once in our lives – and, in fact, some people try to climb it every year. But we also say that if a Japanese person climbs Fuji-san more than once, they are crazy!"

二十九

twenty-nine

Conquering
the Mountain

"**K**eiko-san didn't say anything about climbing this mountain in the dark," Naomi said testily as she and her mother slogged through wet rubble. "I'm sure she had better weather, too."

"It's a good thing we brought raincoats, then, Naomi," Sara replied wearily. They had been climbing for more than four hours. It was three o'clock in the morning and a fine mist had hung over the mountain right from the start. Despite the mist and the early hour, they were not alone; many people had decided to climb Fuji-san on the opening day of climbing season. The trail was busy with hikers who had started late the day before and were climbing through the night, hoping to reach the peak in time for a spectacular sunrise. Naomi knew that other climbers, who had started earlier the day before, were now sleeping in cosy futons at stations seven and eight further up the mountain. The hikers' flashlights cast an eerie glow on the trail. The mood was quiet.

"I'm tired," Naomi said grouchily. She wanted things to get better. They looked at each other glumly. A group of foreigners, who looked like tourists, trudged slowly past them. Several in the group, who obviously hadn't thought about the possibility of rain or mist, were wearing makeshift raincoats fashioned from big garbage bags. They all looked pretty miserable. Just looking at them made Naomi seem more tired than ever.

173

"Do you want to stop, then?" her mother asked, panting, as she found a rock off the main trail and sat down heavily. "It's okay with me. We've been climbing long enough. I should have brought another sweater for each of us. I had no idea it was going to be this cold and wet." She paused for a while and then added, "It's just as well to say we tried. In any case, we can buy the postcard."

Naomi turned and looked back at her mother, surprised. *I know I've been complaining,* she thought, *but it doesn't mean I'm ready to give up! We're not going to give up!* There were three more hours until sunrise and she and her mother were going to see it from the top of Japan's highest mountain. "No, mom. We can do this," Naomi said. It was all she had the strength to say. She turned slowly and began trudging up the mountain without another word.

Sara looked up, surprised. She watched as the small figure of her daughter ascended the trail, falling in line behind the group of older climbers that had just passed. For a moment, the woman wondered how well she knew that little girl – or the person that her little girl had become. "Okay then. Let's do it," Sara said to no one in particular as she pushed herself to her feet. She didn't feel so tired anymore.

More than an hour later, Sara and Naomi took another break by the side of the trail. Naomi's legs ached! Just like Keiko said, the trail was like a steep stairway that just didn't seem to have an end. It rose up into pitch darkness and you couldn't see where it went. Her legs turned to jelly whenever she stopped, even for a second. Her heart pounded in her chest and her breath rasped in her ears. By now, they were taking short breaks every ten minutes. They would stop often, just long enough to take a swallow or two of water.

"According to the trail map," Sara said, "I think we are just below station number eight. One more stop and we're at the top." She trained her flashlight on the trail above. "I think I can see a few small buildings. It must be station eight." ·

"How much further after that?" Naomi asked wearily.

"About another hour?" It was more of a question than a firm response. "I think we're making good time, actually."

Naomi thought so, too. When they took rest breaks, she would notice some of the other climbers go by, only to see them again when they, in turn, stopped to rest at the side of the trail. They were keeping up with the crowd, at least.

"Naomi, do you notice that it is getting lighter?"

Naomi looked up: Her mother was right! She could begin to distinguish shapes. The sky was not black, but more like a deep royal blue. Then she looked down. There were no more twinkling lights from the roads and dwellings below. They had climbed through a layer of clouds. They were above the clouds! Naomi looked up to a sky full of stars.

"It's going to be a wonderful sunrise," Naomi's mother said simply as she put her thermos back inside her rucksack. It was getting even colder, now. She braced herself against the wind, which whipped fiercely.

Feeling energized, they decided to continue walking when they reached the next station, relieved that it would be the last. Naomi shone her flashlight on the buildings and noticed that heavy rocks had been placed on the tin roofs – obviously to keep them from blowing off in the wind! Some climbers were exiting these small inns, looking eager and refreshed after a nice warm rest inside. They were all holding wooden walking sticks and were waiting in line to get them branded. At each station, there was a man who would burn the logo of the station into the wooden walking sticks.

Sara groaned.

Naomi turned, "What is it, mom?" she asked, alarmed.

"Look!" Sara said weakly, and pointed to a sign on one of the small huts.

Naomi looked, and her heart sank. It was a sign, with the number 8.5 written big and black. "Keiko didn't say anything about station eight and a half!" she complained.

"Things change," Sara replied, giving her daughter an encouraging pat on the shoulder. "Let's go."

Naomi focused on the trail ahead and concentrated on lifting her feet up onto every step. One foot, then the other. Then the other again. Then the other. They walked right through station nine without stopping. So focused on her step-climbing, Naomi was taken by surprise when she heard an "Excuse me" just behind her in the now-familiar Japanese accent. Naomi turned around and looked into the smiling eyes of a Japanese man. She peered into his face through the dim light. He was a handsome young man. With a cheerful grin and his hair sticking out of a Yomiuri Giants baseball cap, he could have been someone from the pages of the pop magazines that Ai and Midori loved to read. Naomi stopped to let him pass and stared after him.

He grinned and continued his way up the mountain, never breaking his stride.

"Is that what I think it is?" Naomi asked. She focused her weary eyes again. Her eyes were not deceiving her; the handsome young man was carrying a bicycle on his back. As she looked down the trail to find her mother, another young man came up with a bicycle on his back as well! Naomi waited for her mother to catch up.

"Did you see that?" she cried out in amazement.

"Somehow, it doesn't surprise me," her mother replied breathlessly, shaking her head. "But it kind of puts me to shame." She laughed.

Fifteen minutes later, Naomi heard her mother call out her name, and she turned to see her sitting on a rock by the side of the path. Alarmed, she stepped quickly down the path to her mother.

"Oh, mom! Are you okay?" Naomi asked.

"I'm okay, Naomi. I'm okay. Just tired. All of a sudden, I got tired." Sara looked up, managing a smile. She was panting heavily.

"Mom, we'll go down. We'll have a good rest at station eight and a half, then we'll head back down. Everything's going to be okay," Naomi said, fighting down a panicky feeling.

Sara smiled. She felt she could laugh and cry at the same time, if she weren't so tired. She reached up and ruffled her daughter's hair playfully. "Please don't worry, Naomi. It's not that bad. But I do need to take another break," she said, and then grinned. "Besides, I can't let you do this without me! Let's just have a sit for a little while, okay?"

"Sure, mom," Naomi sat down beside her mother. She grabbed her mother's thermos from her rucksack and poured her mother a drink. Then Naomi reached into her own rucksack and took out a granola bar, broke it in half, and gave her mother a piece. They sat in silence, gazing at the sky. It was getting quite light, now. The sky was taking on a mauve hue. It wouldn't be long before the sun came up at the horizon. Naomi looked up and saw the top of the peak; the ridge of the outer crater. Then she noticed a small dark shape that seemed to be a different colour, perhaps red. The *torii* gate! The end of the trail was close.

"Mom, are you sure you can keep going?" Naomi asked. Sara got up. "Yes, Naomi. I needed that break. But I'm fine, now. Let's go!"

Relieved, Naomi rose and shouldered her rucksack. Mother and daughter continued their trek; one foot up, then the next, then the next ...

The big red Japanese gate loomed larger with each step, until finally, Naomi found herself standing directly under it. She had done it! She had climbed 3,776 metres and was standing on the roof of Japan! She turned around and waited for her mother to climb the final ten metres.

"*Yatta!* – We did it!" Naomi cheered as her mother walked under the gate. She gave her mother a big hug and then took a picture of Sara against the gate.

"Oh, I almost forgot," Sara said as she dug inside the pocket of her anorak. She pulled out a small Canadian flag. "Happy Canada Day, Naomi – although, I suppose, that was yesterday, technically." She handed Naomi the flag. Someone offered to take a picture of them as they posed underneath the gate, Naomi waving the little flag. The sky was changing from mauve to pink, with a broad band of yellow along the eastern horizon. The sunrise wouldn't be much longer, now!

"I'd forgotten how big it is up here," Sara said, surveying the rim.

"Forgotten?" Naomi asked.

"Didn't I tell you? I've climbed Fuji-san before. When I was living in Kyushu," Sara replied off-handedly.

"Why didn't you tell me?"

"Maybe I didn't want you to think I was craaazy," Sara laughed and lunged playfully at her daughter. "Actually, what they say about climbing Fuji-san more than once must be true, but I believe it doesn't apply to us 'outsiders.' Come to think of it, I was feeling pretty crazy for a while – waaay down there," she thrust her chin at the trail below.

Naomi and her mother walked along the road to find an unobstructed view of the morning horizon, and waited, with so many others, for the sun to rise. There were no clouds at the horizon and Naomi could see water all around. She had to remind herself that Japan was an island country and that she was looking out over the vast Pacific Ocean. The wind was strong, and it whipped her hair against her face. Naomi looked up and saw an airplane flying overhead. She wondered where the plane was headed, and felt closer to the passengers in the plane than to the people on earth below.

Naomi and the other climbers put on sunglasses as the sun began its fiery ascent. It shimmered on the water, rose minute by minute, and the sky lightened from mauve to yellow. Naomi heard the click of camera shutters and wondered if anyone thought they could really capture what lay before them. She had long ago stopped trying to capture the sun on film. Sunrises and sunsets were things that she tried to keep in her memory. She tried hard to remember, to picture them in her mind. But it never lasted very long. The only thing Naomi could do was wait for the next opportunity – like this very moment.

"I'm hungry. Let's find some breakfast," her mother said.

"Good idea," Naomi replied and they headed back to the main area. The cute boy with the Yomiuri Giants baseball cap rode by on his bicycle. He flashed a grin at Naomi.

"Hello!" he said, and waved. Naomi giggled.

"Now, there's a guy who looks like he's climbed this mountain too many times," Sara joked. Then she shook her head, looked down at her daughter and sighed happily. "We deserve – " she began, searching for what to say next. "We deserve the biggest bowl of *ramen* on top of this mountain."

"What's the highest mountain in the world?"

"Everest."

"And who climbed it first?"

"Sir Edmund Hillary."

"And – what did he say?"

"That's an unfair question! I'll bet he said many things."

"Yes, I'll bet he did, too. But he also said: We don't conquer the mountain. We conquer ourselves."

"Yeah, we did. We did it – didn't we."

 thirty

A Special Wish

Naomi rose early and went to the window. Despite the early hour, the sun was already hot. But a crisp Hokkaido breeze was blowing nicely, tempering the heat. It was going to be a good day for Naomi's special surprise. Only her mother and Takenaka-sensei knew about it, and she was especially grateful to Takenaka-sensei for helping her get it organized. This surprise was going to be her way of saying thank you to all her friends in Pippu-cho. Naomi went over to her desk and surveyed her checklist – all the items needed had been bought in advance, and Baba and Gigi had mailed some of them weeks earlier. Her timetable of things to do was in order. *Just hope nothing goes wrong*, Naomi thought as she read over her list again, just to be sure. She knew she had a lot of work to do. But first, there was some other important business to attend to. Today, she and Keiko would have their last official study session on Japanese customs and traditions, and Naomi had something in particular she wanted to know about.

After breakfast, Naomi and Keiko were enjoying some cold barley tea on the balcony looking out over the rice field and the potato fields. "Please tell me about *Tanabata*, Keiko-san." Naomi asked eagerly.

"Ah, yes, of course – today is July 7. *Tanabata* – the Star Festival. What do you know about it?" Keiko asked.

"Well, I know *Tanabata* is today. I saw it marked on my calendar,"

Naomi smiled. "I know that towns and cities across Japan will have festivals today, and they'll make wishes. But I'm not sure why it is called a Star Festival."

"You're right, Naomi. Today, all across Japan, people will be going to these festivals to make wishes. We always have a big festival in the grounds of the big shrine near the Pippu Town Hall. We make a wish to the stars *Orihime* and *Hikoboshi* – Vega and Altair, you say in English – and hope that our wishes will be granted." Keiko paused to take another sip of cold barley tea.

"In Japanese lore, we have a special legend about the stars Vega and Altair. Millions of years ago, when the galaxy was being formed, Vega and Altair were in love with each other. They were very close. But when the Milky Way was being formed, it grew between the two stars. These two star-crossed sweethearts became separated by the Milky Way. They wished forever to be together again."

"That's a nice story, in a way," Naomi declared.

"I agree. And when we celebrate the *Tanabata* Festival, we hope that the two stars will grant us our own small wishes." Keiko smiled and added, "Of course, as you know, we often go to temples or shrines across the country, asking for good fortune in all kinds of things; health, wealth, happiness – "

"Good grades at school," Naomi added, remembering her visit to a shrine with Kiyoka some time ago.

Keiko nodded, "You're right. But at *Tanabata*, we have an interesting custom. At the festival site, many bamboo branches will be driven into the ground, like little trees. We write our wishes on small pieces of coloured paper, and then hang them on the bamboo branches with pieces of string."

Naomi looked out at the vivid green rice field before them. She tried hard to place that same colour back on the Manitoba prairie.

"We don't have that colour where I come from," she said simply.

Keiko looked at the rice field, and then to Naomi. Her eyes sparkled, "No. But I wonder if we have the blue of your famous prairie sky."

Naomi thought about it. "No. You don't," she replied with a smile.

"Someday, I hope to see this famous big sky country that your mother always talked about," Keiko said.

Naomi and her mother drove up to the temple grounds in the minivan that they'd borrowed for the day. They began to unload the van. "We'll have to make several trips — it's a good things the tents are not too far away," Sara said. For a moment, a look of worry crossed her face and she looked at Naomi. "We'd better get started."

Naomi grinned. Everything was going to be all right. She knew it. "We can do it, mom."

Sara's gaze rested on her daughter for some time. "Naomi," she began, "I want to tell you that this idea of yours is the best thing we could have done to say thank you to everyone here. I never would have thought of it, myself. So, thank you, Naomi. I'm proud of you."

"Thanks, mom," Naomi replied happily. She picked up some boxes and headed toward the tents that were being assembled along the walkway leading to the entrance of Pippu-cho's largest shrine. People were busy setting up their wares. There were stalls of ceramic dishes and fresh produce. Some people would be selling *yakisoba* — fried noodles. Naomi noticed a cotton candy stall, and a couple who would be selling goldfish from two small plastic wading pools. She grimaced when she saw the *yaki-ika* fried squid-on-a-stick stall being set up. Naomi had tried, but just couldn't get used to eating grilled squid on a stick, even if it was one of the most popular foods to eat at festivals like this.

"Over here, Naomi!" Naomi saw Takenaka-sensei struggling with the pipe frame of their tent. Walking as fast as she could, Naomi went over to help. She put her boxes on the table in front of the tent, and reached to steady one of the pipes.

"Naomi, I am excited about this. I almost told Midori — almost," Takenaka-sensei said, and winked. "All the schools in Pippu-cho will finish early today, so the children can take part in the *Tanabata* Festival. I think people will start coming around noon."

Naomi looked inside the small tent area, and then went around and circled the tent. She returned to the front where Takenaka-sensei and her mother were standing. At once, Sara noticed the worried look on Naomi's face.

"What's wrong?" Naomi's mother asked.

Naomi took a deep breath, "Takenaka-sensei, did you forget — "

Takenaka-sensei's grin vanished. "The Mountie! I forgot the Mountie!"

Since May, when Naomi had first asked Mr. Takenaka for his help, Naomi had been spending a little time each week painting a picture of an RCMP officer on a horse, proudly holding a Canadian flag. She had finished it only a week before leaving for Fuji-san, and then Takenaka-sensei had carefully cut an oval shape where the Mountie's head was supposed to be. He had offered to store it at his school.

"I'll go to the school in the van and get it, no problem," her mother said. "Don't worry, Naomi." A look of relief quickly spread across both Naomi's and Takenaka-sensei's faces.

A big banner stretched across the top of the stall that read: *Portage la Prairie, Manitoba – Strawberry Capital of Canada!* in big red letters. At each end, Naomi had painted two big strawberries with happy faces and little arms and legs, holding Canadian flags. Around the outside of the tent, she had pinned several large posters from the Canadian Embassy in Tokyo. Each poster depicted a region of Canada: the Arctic, the Maritimes, the Prairies, Ontario, Quebec, and British Columbia. The posters had lovely photographs and the text was written in Japanese. Off to the side, they had set up the large plywood picture of the faceless RCMP officer on his trusty black stallion. Naomi knew people would enjoy having their picture taken as a genuine Canadian Mountie!

In front of the stall, on a long, narrow table, Naomi and her mother had set up the three frying pans. They were going to make pancakes with real Canadian maple syrup. Behind the table, Naomi had placed boxes of maple-leaf shaped candies and cookies, as well as a box of small Canada flag pins. She would give these away.

A delivery man, his arms loaded with several trays of strawberries, was coming down the walkway. Sara motioned him over and took the boxes from him. He smiled and bowed as he accepted his payment, looking at the stall with interest.

"Making strawberry pancakes is a nice touch," Naomi's mother said.

Naomi nodded. "Well, I think it's neat that strawberries are important to both Pippu-cho and Portage," she replied. "But mainly, it's in honour of the nickname the kids at Pippu Elementary School gave me. I hope some of them will come."

"I'm sure they will," Sara replied. "After all, *Tanabata* is an important festival – and who wouldn't want to meet the Strawberry

Blonde of Pippu-cho?" She grinned and hugged her daughter.

Naomi noticed that some of the other stall operators were beginning to linger by her stall, looking with curiosity at the posters she had taped to the sides of the tent. A rather large woman caught Naomi's eye and motioned to the frying pan with a shy smile.

"Su-to-ro-be-ri pan-cake," Naomi said, and tipped a little pancake mix into a frypan while her mother quickly washed and cut a box of strawberries. Within minutes, Naomi had flipped the pancake onto a paper plate and added some syrup. She handed the plate, along with a pair of chopsticks, to the woman and said, "Here you are!"

The woman took a tentative bite. Naomi knew that, for many people, maple syrup was an acquired taste. Some found it too sweet. She didn't need to worry; the woman's eyebrows shot up in approval as she quickly ate the rest of the pancake. "*Ikura desuka?* – How much does it cost?" the woman asked.

Naomi smiled. She wasn't selling anything. This was a gift to the people of Pippu-cho – her chance to say thank you to everyone. She replied, "Sa-bi-su," and waved her hand from side to side. This was a common word in Japanese, meaning, as it sounded, "service" and was a way of saying that something was complimentary or free of charge.

The woman bowed her head slightly. "Very good," she said in a thick Japanese accent. She laughed at her own funny-sounding English and walked away. Sara and Naomi looked at her and then at each other, and smiled.

"Mom, can you take over for a couple of minutes, please? There's something I want to do," Naomi asked. She lifted off her apron, emblazoned with a large red maple leaf, and headed for the shrine. It was the largest and oldest shrine in Pippu-cho, and the most popular one. At its side, Naomi could see a line of tall bamboo branches set firmly into the ground. Already, several *Tanabata* "wishes" were hanging on the branches. Carefully pulling a square of coloured origami paper out of her pocket, Naomi tied it to a branch.

When she returned to the tent, the crowds were beginning to arrive. Soon, she and her mother were working steadily. It wasn't long before Ai and Kiyoka came running up to the stall, breathless with excitement, followed by most of the English Club. Ai was pulling her little brother Makoto and her mother behind her. In a flash, the two girls were in the back of the tent, helping Naomi whip up another batch of pancake mix. Soon, Midori, Takenaka-sensei and his wife arrived. With them was Miss Ichimiya and the entire class from Pippu Elementary School. The children were lined up in rows and holding onto ropes to stay together.

"Waaaaaa! Naomi-sensei! Su-to-ro-be-ri pan-cake!" Naomi heard the children cry out in delight.

"Strawberry pancakes and maple candies for everyone!" Naomi cried out as Sara, Ai and Kiyoka began handing plates to all the children. They nodded their approval as they ate the pancakes. Miss Ichimiya passed a box she was holding to Hiroyuki. He walked up to Naomi and lifted the box up to her.

Naomi laughed at the smears of strawberry on Hiroyuki's face as she took the box. "What is it?" she asked.

"Open it Naomi-sensei!" the children cried out in excitement.

Naomi carefully opened the box and looked in. Her eyes were wide and her mouth was a perfect "o" as she pulled out a large paper bundle: a thousand paper cranes, strung together in one large multicoloured bundle. She looked all around her. There was Keiko, Midori, Takenaka-sensei and his wife, Miss Ichimiya and the whole class, Ai and Kiyoka and her friends from school. *They're all here*, she thought happily.

"Let's take a group photo with the Mountie," said Takenaka-sensei. He held up his camera and motioned for everyone to crowd in around the big picture.

"Who will be the Canadian Mountie?" one of the children asked in Japanese. Everyone laughed as they looked at the empty hole over the Mountie's face. A man walked up and took Takenaka-sensei's camera, motioning for him to get into the picture. Everyone laughed as the principal pretended to protest, and then happily walked behind the big board to stick his face through the hole.

"Cheezu!" everyone yelled out, as the picture was taken.

"I want a copy of that picture," Naomi called out to Takenaka-sensei.

"No problem!"

Naomi passed out Canada pins to the group and then returned to the table to make more pancakes. For two more hours, a steady stream of friends and neighbours came by to sample the Canadian food.

And when it was all gone, they stayed to talk, and read the posters about Canada. Naomi was surprised to know just how much people knew about her and her mother. Some of them told Naomi how they remembered seeing her in the store one day months back, or out on her bicycle, or in the park with her frends. *It's just like Portage la Prairie*, she thought.

Later that evening, Naomi lay snuggled in her summer futon. She thought about the wish she had written on the coloured paper and tied to the bamboo branch, and smiled. The Star Festival had been a success. Her wish had been granted.

三十一

thirty-one

A New Beginning

Keiko, Naomi, and her mother walked along the underground passage to platform four, where the train taking them to Sapporo, and then to Morioka, would come in. In Morioka, a city at the northern end of Japan's largest island of Honshu, Naomi and her mother would catch the super-high-speed train bound for Tokyo. They would arrive in Tokyo early the next morning and then head to Tokyo International Airport at Narita. From there, it was an eight-hour flight by jumbo jet to Vancouver, and then home to Winnipeg.

Baba and Gigi will be waiting for us at Winnipeg International Airport. There isn't much time to go. It's hard to believe that a whole year has come and gone. I can't believe I'm leaving Pippu-cho. All these thoughts tumbled through Naomi's mind as she struggled with her heavy suitcase and her rucksack. Not even winning the haiku contest yesterday, scoring the double-header with Midori that Naomi had felt sure she wouldn't be able to do, could bring a smile to her face this morning.

Keiko and Sara were also carrying heavy bags and, as they walked, Sara apologized repeatedly to the older woman for the burden. Naomi wasn't listening. She put her bags down and looked at her watch. It was 7:15 a.m. The train to Sapporo was going to leave in ten minutes. Where was Kiyoka, Midori and Ai?

"Don't worry, Naomi. They'll be here," Sara said. "Maybe they're already on the platform."

Naomi shouldered her rucksack, picked up her suitcase and followed her mother and Keiko up the stairs to the railway platform. She looked up and saw several people milling around, waiting for the train to arrive. But she saw no familiar faces, and a lump formed in her throat. As Naomi reached the top step, she let her bag fall with a thump to the concrete floor of the platform. She felt she couldn't breathe.

A rumbling little giggle rose to a familiar guffaw. Naomi whirled around on the platform, just as Hiroyuki and his friends jumped out from inside the platform waiting room. All at once there was a cacophony of voices; "Goodbye Miss Naomi!" "Su-to-ro-be-ri-sensei!" "Sayonara!" Naomi heard these words above the happy din. Miss Ichimiya was there, too. More than half the class had come out early to say goodbye to Naomi for the last time. Hiroyuki danced around the platform with his fingers up to his temples, impersonating a little devil - just like he had done on her birthday. Naomi smiled. *I'll never forget that day*, she thought. She moved forward to ruffle Hiroyuki's hair, and he hugged her, his eyes looking up at her and his chin resting on her stomach. Before she knew what was happening, all the children had surrounded her in a big group bear hug that was threatening to take her off her feet!

Takenaka-sensei and his wife came up the stairs to the platform. The scrum broke up as the principal walked over to Naomi and handed her a photo. It was the one from the Star Festival, of everyone standing by the Mountie.

"Thank you, Takenaka-sensei," Naomi said as she placed the photo carefully in her rucksack. She looked up at him and asked, "Where's Midori?" Takenaka-sensei glanced at his wife and smiled a little smile. He scratched his head and shrugged. Naomi didn't understand what was going on. She looked at her watch. *Five minutes left! Where are they?*

The clock over platform four moved another minute closer to departure. The train was approaching. Naomi could see the light far down the track. She looked at Keiko and her mother. How could she leave without saying goodbye to her three best friends?

"Look, Naomi! They're here!" Keiko said and pointed over Naomi's shoulder. Naomi turned to see her friends Kiyoka, Midori and Ai running the length of the platform from the stairway, with the entire English Club running to catch up! She noticed that Kiyoka, Midori, and Ai each seemed to be holding something small in their hands. As they drew closer, Kiyoka held the object out in front of her. It was a small red book.

"Passu porto!" Breathless, Ai said it first. It was a brand new Japanese passport. All three girls had one. Naomi took Kiyoka's passport and opened it. There was Kiyoka's smiling face. She looked over at Ai and Kiyoka and then up at her mother and Keiko. It could mean only one thing.

"The adventure isn't over yet, Naomi," her mother said simply.

"We're coming to Canada!" Midori cried jubilantly.

"When?" Naomi was almost speechless.

"August!" Ai and Midori said in unison.

"Wha – ?" Naomi didn't know what to say.

Naomi's mother laughed. "It's true, Naomi. August 8th. For three weeks. Baba and Gigi have invited them. And Keiko and I have convinced their parents that you'll help them improve their English." Sara gave her daughter a mock serious look and said, "You've got work to do."

It was too good to be true, but true it was. Naomi whooped with joy and hugged the three girls. People began to board the train which had pulled in. The conductor was helping Sara with their bags. It was really time to go.

Naomi turned to the English Club, Miss Ichimiya, the children, and to Mr. and Mrs. Takenaka. "*Honto ni, domo arigato gozaimashita* - Really, thank you so much," she began. She looked across at everyone's smiling faces and the lump returned to her throat. She struggled for words. *How do I thank them all for their kindness, their friendship? The past year in Japan has been the best year of my life.* Naomi knew she had been scared when she first arrived in Pippu-cho, but those feelings were so far away, now.

"Goodbye, Naomi," Miss Ichimiya said, and waved. Her students repeated after her in a familiar chorus. "Keep in touch," she added.

Impulsively, Naomi reached over to give her a hug, then found herself hugging Takenaka-sensei and his wife, and eveyone else. Midori, Kiyoka, and Ai crowded around her and they huddled together. Naomi laughed giddily when she saw Ai give Kiyoka a big bear hug, clowning as always.

Then, Naomi turned to Keiko. She rushed into the woman's arms as her face crumpled into a sob. The older woman stroked her hair and whispered into her ear. "Do your best. I will see you soon."

"*Winnipeg de aimashoo!*" Ai cried out.

"Meet you in Winnipeg!" Midori translated proudly. All of a sudden, her face froze, and her hands shook as she struggled to open her school bag. She pulled out a box and thrust it into Naomi's hands, pushing her up onto the steps of the train as she did so.

There was no time left. "I'll be waiting at the airport!" Naomi called out, to reassure them, as she backed up into the train. The buzzer was sounding. The train began to pull away.

Naomi walked quickly ahead into the seating area of the train and took the empty seat by the window next to her mother. She pressed her hand on the glass. As the train pulled out of the station, everyone began to wave again. Midori, Kiyoka and Ai walked alongside the train and quickly found themselves jogging to keep up, waving their precious new passports.

"Bye," Naomi said softly as the train picked up speed. The girls stopped at the end of the platform and continued to wave as their three figures became smaller and smaller. Then the train turned a corner, and they were gone. Naomi fell back in her seat. For several moments, she sat and stared straight ahead, barely able to breathe. Then she looked down at the box in her lap, as if noticing it for the first time. Slowly, she lifted the lid. It was the Daruma doll. Naomi smiled. Both eyes were painted in, now.

Naomi rested her head against the window. She was looking out over green hills and rice paddies, now. Soon the crows would be calling, hoping for a little bit of rice straight from the stalk. The girl smiled as she felt a tear roll down her cheek. "I'll come back," she whispered to herself. "This is my story. I will live it every day."

Naomi's Favourite Websites About Japan

Hiroshima Peace Site:
www.city.hiroshima.jp/peacesite

Kidsweb Japan
www.jinjapan.org/kidsweb

Sadako Peace Project:
www.sadako.org

Sapporo Snow Festival Official Home Page:
www.aurora-net.or.jp/~snowfes/index.html

Naomi's Favourite Books About Japan

An Introduction to Haiku,
by R. Blythe (Kodansha)

The Adventure of Momotaro, the Peach boy,
by Ralph F. McCarthy (Kodansha)

Grass Sandals: The Travels of Basho,
by Dawnine Spivak (Athenium)

Lily and Wooden Bowl,
by Alan Schroeder, Yoriko Ito (Picture Yearling)

Remembering the Kanji,
by James W. Heisig (Japan Publications)

Sadako and the Thousand Paper Cranes,
by Eleanor Coerr (Putnam)

Totto-chan: The Little Girl at the Window,
by Tetsuko Kuroyanagi (Kodansha)

About the Author

Karmel Schreyer lives in Hong Kong with her husband and is a writer of educational materials for Asian children. She is the daughter of former Governor General Edward Schreyer. Karmel has lived in Paris, Florence, Canberra, Tokyo, Yogjakarta and Hong Kong. She taught English for three years in Japan, and drew inspiration from her own experiences there for *Naomi: The Strawberry Blonde of Pippu Town,* which is her first novel.